not so kind regards

WARTS & CLAWS INC. SERIES

CLIO EVANS

Copyright © 2022 Clio Evans

Cover illustrated by @poppypari (instagram)

All rights reserved. No part of this book may be reproduced or used in any manner without the prior written permission of the copyright owner, except for the use of brief quotations in a book review.

"An office is for not dying. An office is a place to live life to the fullest, to the max, to... an office is a place where dreams come true." — Michael Scott, The Office

warning!

HR Department:

Dear Reader,
There have been **R**eports of the following in this office: tail fucking, voyeurism, use of office supplies for pleasure, corporate lingo, inappropriate behavior between coworkers, sexting, cum drinking, spanking, BDSM, Domme/sub dynamics, omega heats, interesting anatomy, degradation, and more.

If any of this makes you uncomfortable, please report it to your HR rep immediately.

Not So Kind Regards—
Warts & Claws Horn-y Resources

CHAPTER ONE
witches get bitches

INFERNA

"Where the fuck is my coffee?" I huffed, picking up the phone on my desk.

I smashed in the receptionist's number, my tail flicking with annoyance.

Morning light poured into my office, filtering through the shiny windows. I could see the whole city from here and it was moments like this that I liked to twirl around and stare while growling at my receptionist.

"Yes, Miss Inferna?" Anne asked on the line, her tone pleasant and chipper.

Very deceiving too. Anne was Medusa's granddaughter, and on a bad day recently, I'd had to file an incident report because her snakes had ripped into one of the new guys for talking shit about how she answered the phones. I had no idea how she'd come to be, but I didn't ask questions when it came to monsters and their parents.

"I thought my coffee was supposed to be here," I said, drumming my fingers on my thigh.

I was wearing a very nice tailored suit, my blazer prim with an expensive silk blouse beneath it.

I was the boss, and the boss wanted coffee.

"Well..." Anne drifted off, her voice taking on the tinny sound of someone who didn't want to explain why I was still waiting on my sacred brew. "You see...the witches took the coffee maker this morning."

"The *what*?" I asked, spinning back around to glare at the door to my office.

"The witches. The Warts' boss, Mr. Snakeroot, came in this morning. He got here before you did, and he took our coffee maker. He said theirs broke. I tried to stop him, but he..."

"He *what*, Anne?" I hissed.

"He said that you were always late and wouldn't notice anyway."

"Funny. Because I'm noticing now, Anne."

"Yes, I know."

"Not only am I noticing, but I was also early today."

"Yes, I know, Miss Inferna."

"For god's sake," I cursed, slamming the phone down.

I reached forward and logged off my computer, jumping out of my chair.

If the witches wanted a fight with us monsters, then they would get one. I was done playing pretend, acting like I didn't notice their stupid antics. They'd been fucking with my floor for too long.

We all worked in the same building, our companies renting different levels to do our work. My floor was dedicated to Claws Inc., which was the company I'd joined fresh out of school. We worked with different social media companies, helping them solve bug problems within the new filters that were being developed specifically for monsters. Wanted to hide your big bad teeth? Your scales and horns? We had filters that could do that. We hired monsters exclusively, ones that wanted to get acclimated to the human world.

Then there were the witches.

We were the only two supernatural offices in the god damned city, and somehow we'd ended up in the same building.

I still had no idea what the Warts did and didn't give a fuck. What I did know was that when they had moved in three months ago, there had been annoying little things here and there. Elevators taking monsters to the wrong floor, toilets flushing non-stop, doors locking for no reason. Ink turning invisible.

Petty witch shit.

I straightened my blazer and pants and then walked out of my office, my heels clicking on the hardwoods. My door flew open and I stepped out, taking a look around at everyone.

"Good morning, Claws," I said, offering them all a wicked smile.

Poppins, a griffin shifter who liked to wear plaid and a good friend, gave a low whistle. "What'd they do today, Boss?" He cracked his knuckles, claws glinting like razors.

"Took my fucking coffee machine," I barked, marching through the cubicles.

A couple of snickers, a couple of growls, a couple of '*get em's*. I kept my shoulders back and my head high as I passed the front desk and left our office.

"Do you want backup?" One of the wolf boys called.

"No, I think I can handle a couple of witches," I answered, heading straight for the elevator.

I punched the button, waiting for the doors to slide open. I stepped inside, glaring at my reflection in the silver.

I was about to hang a witch by his balls. Daddy would be proud.

Well, one of them would.

I smirked a little, thinking about my dads. One of them was an incubus through and through while the other was a human. I was a perfect blend of them both, although I definitely took more after my creature daddy. My brother took more after my papa. Very nice, very sweet, very *not* hang a witch by their balls because they stole your coffee pot.

The elevator dinged and I was immediately met with the scent of witches. It smelled like herbs and potions on this floor and I wrinkled my nose as I stepped into the hall.

I knew right where Mr. Snakeroot was.

I marched towards their door and slid inside, not even sparing a glance at their receptionist.

"Ma'am!" I heard her call. "Ma'am! You can't just walk in!"

I paused, twisting to look at her. I pointed one of my sharp black nails at her, "It seems like my legs are working just fine, Sally. But maybe you should sit back down before I turn you into my office pet."

There was a collective gasp and I felt the air thrum with anger. Sally's mouth parted and I saw the flicker there. The lust.

Ohhh, yeah. I smirked, my tail flicking. I often forgot how much power I had over humans, even witches. I looked like sex on a stick to them and even if Sally was happily married with three kids, she would still lick the bottom of my Pradas if I told her to.

I ignored the swiveling heads as I marched straight to *his* office.

I opened the door and slammed it behind me.

The sight before me was one I would have enjoyed in a different setting, but the way Mr. Snakeroot's mouth dropped with a snarl was worth walking in on regardless.

"WHAT THE FUCK?"

I arched a brow, taking in everything.

One of his little office witches was bent over the desk, his hands bound with his tie. Mr. Snakeroot's pants were down, his cock most definitely buried inside of his little witch.

He let out a squeal, trying to move, but his boss pinned him there. His eyes sparked with fury, burning like blue hellfire.

Mr. Snakeroot was pissed.

I smiled, amused. I crossed his office to MY coffee pot that sat on one of the little drink bars against the wall. I plucked what could only be his favorite cup, one that said 'WITCHES GET BITCHES', and poured myself a steaming cup of brew.

"You need to leave," Mr. Snakeroot huffed. "I'm a little busy."

"No, no," I purred, waltzing back to the two of them.

The little witch's eyes widened in fear as I dragged up one of the chairs and plopped down, making sure they could both see me. His glamor made him look like a pretty golden man, but I could see beneath it and I liked seeing the little monster get railed by his boss. I raised the cup to my lips, taking a sip of god's brew.

I smiled a little at the red lip stain that was left. Fuck, there was a part of me that wanted to mark every fucking item in this office just to piss the witchy boss off.

"Don't stop because of me, Mr. Snakeroot. I'd hate to get between you and your new client. Or maybe I'd like to be there, he's kind of cute," I said, dropping my voice to one of seduction.

His face reddened and I knew his cock had hardened too.

"Stop," the little witch cried. "Let me up, Arthur. We weren't supposed to get caught. We had spells up!"

I glanced back at the door, seeing the shimmer. I frowned, wondering how I had passed straight through that.

This building was weird at times.

"Spells or no spells— you know the whole office has ears right?" I chuckled, crossing my legs. "I bet some of your wizards get off to hearing you squeal like a speared pig, little witchling."

"God damn it," Mr. Snakeroot cursed. He pulled out of him, pulling up his pants.

His rage was enough to make the air shimmer. I watched the two of them rearrange themselves and then took an obnoxiously loud sip of my coffee as the little witch threw his boss's tie at him, put on his glasses and straightened his clothes, and ran out of the office.

The door slammed behind us, leaving me alone with the very disheveled boss of Warts Co.

"*What the fuck do you want?*" he snarled, planting his hands on the desk.

I studied him, *really* studied him. He was handsome, his dark hair cut nice, his shoulders broad, his skin tan. He had a neatly trimmed beard, the kind that I liked to play with. He had an air of power about him, the snobby aura of a witch.

"Well, this morning, I arrived at my office at 7:55 a.m.

and I called my assistant. 'Where is my coffee?' I asked. You know what Anne told me?" I asked, keeping my tone painfully polite and professional, "She told me that Mr. Snakeroot borrowed my trusty pot. So I just came to get a cup from my own coffee pot that should have been in my own office. And I also got a little breakfast with it too," I said, grinning.

I didn't bother trying to hide my sharp teeth. I didn't fight the dark part of me, the one that very much wished I could feed off both him and the little scared blonde who'd run for the hills. The cute little blonde.

I felt my body hum for a moment, but I tried to ignore it. The way that little witch's eyes had widened had been way too fucking cute. I was way too hungry to be around this right now, but still.

I would need to book an appointment to feed so I didn't pick off these two. The air was enough to keep me sated, their hormones giving me a breath of fresh air.

His gaze darkened, his lips twisting into a snarl. "This is unprofessional."

"*This* is? Or would you say that fucking one of your employees and having a coffee cup that says 'WITCHES GET BITCHES' is? What do you think HR would say, Mr. Snakeroot?"

I leaned forward, enjoying the taste of electricity in the air.

"You think just because you're a monster that you're powerful," he whispered, glaring at me. "But witches have always been stronger than you stupid heathens. I could fry you right now and eat you up."

"And I could step on your puny cock and fuck you with my tail," I said, slamming his mug down on the edge of his desk.

I rose, planting my hands opposite of him. I leaned in, enjoying the scent of...arousal?

I swallowed hard, ignoring my thirst. "I don't care what issues you have with monsters, Mr. Snakeroot. But I do care about you messing with my office. We work on separate floors. We work for separate companies. And I'd hate to see yours accidentally catch on fire."

"I'd hate to see you end up with ink spilled on your pretty blouse," he sneered.

"I'd hate to see you stapled to the fucking wall with a demon cock down your throat."

His poker face was good. Too good. My words settled between us and I watched him visibly collect himself, his rage melting into caramel-coated words.

"Inferna, is it?" he asked, shifting his tone. He went from being a rogue to...incredibly charming.

"Ms. Inferna. I'm the Ops of Claws Inc."

"I'm the Ops Leader of Warts Co. in this region. I think we've gotten off on the wrong foot," he said, slowly standing straight up.

"Indeed." I was confused by this shift in professionalism. One minute, he was practically feral. Now, he was the picture-perfect boss.

"I apologize for taking your coffee maker. It was my intention to bring it back. I thought there was another coffee maker in your office."

"This one was a gift from my uncle who owns a coffee shop and it means something to me," I said, straightening my back.

Now, he stared at me. His eyes roamed shamelessly down my body, pausing to take in my tail and crimson skin.

"A succubus, right?"

"That's a bit rude of you," I snapped. "But, yes."

"I apologize. I'm a witch, I see what I see. And right now I'd like to see you take your coffee maker and leave, peacefully. Preferably without seducing my entire office and without sending Sally into a tailspin."

I snorted but still smirked. My gaze took him in for a moment and I realized that he was, in fact, still painfully hard and that the tip of his cock was poking through his zipper.

I arched a brow, intrigued. He didn't have a normal human dick, it seemed.

I licked my lips, wishing that my thoughts weren't becoming dirty.

I hated this fucker.

"I'd like for you to zip up your fly, Mr. Snakeroot."

His hand immediately fell to his crotch and he winced.

With that, I spun on my heels and grabbed the coffee maker from the table. I balanced the machine on one hip and held the half-full pot with my free hand.

"Wait! Can I at least get a cup?"

I didn't even spare him a glance as I opened up his office door with my tail. "You can finish mine. Good boys take whatever they can get."

I then marched through their office, not giving the glares and wide eyes a second look. I caught a glimpse of the little witchling settling into his desk, his eyes very much avoiding me and his cheeks bright red.

I snorted, slid out into the hall, hopped on my elevator, and went back to my floor.

The moment I walked in with the coffee maker, the entire office cheered.

"Did you skin him?" Anne asked happily, her eyes burning with dark delight.

"No, but I don't think he'll come back here," I chuckled,

setting the maker down back in its spot. It was the holy grail of our office, a place where we could all take a moment to fuel up.

The office was chattering, all fifteen monsters talking about our victory.

"Alright, creatures," I said, raising my voice. "Let's knock our shit out today and go home. I'm about to be joining a meeting and then I'll be joining in."

Another cheer and I slinked back to my office, fresh coffee in my hands.

The witches wouldn't fuck with us again.

CHAPTER TWO
fangtastic monday

ART

I could practically hear the Claws office cheer through the fucking walls upon their boss's arrival. I groaned, leaning forward in my chair.

My cock was hard and needy. I hadn't finished fucking Calen, and now he was embarrassed and pissed. Inferna had ruined everything.

Fucking hell. I hadn't even had my own coffee yet because he'd pounced on me the moment I'd walked through the doors with the machine.

I glared across my desk, seeing Inferna's cup. Her crimson lipstick stained the rim, and a part of me wanted to lick it off.

That woman was trouble. A goddess of sin, a walking, talking, breathing version of sex. I'd been so mad once I'd seen her waltz in like she owned me— but there was a small part of me that enjoyed that.

A very small part of me wanted to find out what her tail could do to me.

A knock at the door had me scooting my chair up, hiding my boner under my desk. I waved my fingers through the air, the little burst of magic pulling the door open.

"Good morning," Sally said, still entirely too flustered. "This morning has been... eventful. But, everything is still on schedule, and we should have a productive day."

"Great," I growled, trying not to scowl. "Can we add a coffee maker to the list of things we need?"

"Yes, sir," Sally said. She cleared her throat, shifting from foot to foot.

"What is it, Sally?" I asked.

"It's just... It's just that my tarot deck had omens in it this morning, sir. And I feel the need to warn you about that succubus."

"Warn me about her how?" I asked, shaking my head. "The Claws office has nothing to do with us. I didn't ask permission to use their coffee maker, which is why she marched down here."

"Yes, well," Sally hissed, her purple eyes flickering. "None of us like those monsters. Still, I feel like I should warn you. She won't be good for you."

"Thanks, Sally," I grit out, my cock still pulsing.

How fucking long would I be hard for that sexy monster?

"Can you send Calen in, please?" I asked. "And then I will be joining the conference on new processes rolled out to us from corporate."

"Yes, sir," she said.

I fought the urge to sigh, trying to paint on a perfect face. "Great. Well, I will go ahead and enjoy the rest of this cup of coffee and then will be in meetings. Calen will be here for the first one and then check on everyone's audits. Please send an email out notifying everyone that we will have a team meeting at the end of today, after lunch."

"Will do," Sally said, giving me a curt nod.

She marched out of the office with that, leaving me to stew in my mental cauldron of grumpiness.

I shouldn't have been fucking Calen here, to begin with. Things were already complicated enough, and hiding the feelings coming up between us was getting harder to do.

I was pretty certain everyone in the office knew what we were doing. Calen and I got here early often, and I'd become used to fucking him over my desk.

Still, I kept him at arm's length. It was hard to let anyone close, and I'd be a fucking liar if I tried to pretend that I didn't use his own flaws to my advantage.

My laptop dinged, and I opened it just as Calen entered the doorway. He slowly shut the door behind him, the silence settling between us.

I was pissed that he had run away and left me with Inferna. Not only that, he had squealed like a god damn pig.

Not *only* that, he had gotten so much fucking harder with her sitting there watching us like the queen of the castle.

"Is my cock not enough for you?" I asked, finally succumbing and taking a sip of the coffee cup Inferna had left.

"What the fuck do you mean?" Calen snapped, walking over to me. He plopped in the chair, fixing the cuffs of his button-down.

Looking at him while he had a glamor on, he looked like a pretty blonde businessman. One that was sleek and charming, smart and driven. His brown turtle glasses were sharp, magnifying the gold of his eyes. He primarily wore pastel blues and khaki, his choices in clothing always pushing into more business than casual.

Meanwhile, there had been days occasionally that I would show up in jeans and a t-shirt versus the suit I wore now.

"You got hard while she was watching," I said, taking a sip.

Calen snorted. "I'd be a fucking liar if I didn't admit to wanting her. I don't hold the same hate most of you have for monsters. I've been with monsters in bed, Art, and they're fucking good. Especially when they have a tail or horns or— I wonder what her pussy would—"

"Calen," I snarled, glaring at him.

"What if her pussy is monstrous?"

"Calen, I swear to the gods that I will boil you alive."

"You can punish me in other ways, you know," he chuckled.

My cock pulsed, his tone alone making me hard. "We didn't finish what we started. And now, I only have fifteen minutes before one of my meetings and succubus lipstick-stained coffee. Also, I don't want to hear another thing out of your mouth about her. The Claws office is our enemy."

Calen arched a golden brow. "I'm here to take notes, aren't I? I can take them from under your desk."

"We need to try and focus," I huffed, shifting in my seat.

Calen grinned, and his body shimmered, his true form appearing for just a moment.

Some witches were really more like monsters, and he was one of them. It had never bothered me, in fact...

"Calen," I muttered, my voice hoarse. "Fuck."

There was something irresistible about him right now, and I could not put my finger on it. Even though we had been doing this for some time, I needed him right now.

Which was why I had been pounding into him on my desk earlier. There was a need, a lust...

Part of me wondered if there was something else to it, but that thought flew straight out of my mind as Calen flicked his fingers. I heard the office door lock, his magic throwing up a sound barrier.

Both of us had become very well versed in the spell of silence.

He let his glamor fall, revealing himself completely. Without the cloak of a golden businessman, he had deep emerald skin with shimmering flecks. His hair was a deep black, and his teeth sharpened— just like that bossy succubus'.

I liked the feeling of those teeth scraping over my ridged cock as he sucked me.

What I enjoyed most was the way his body glimmered when he used magic in his true form. He was beautiful, stunning— and I really needed to finish fucking him before I lost my god damned mind.

"Goddess," I whispered. "Get on your knees, I'm going to fuck your throat, and you're going to swallow every drop."

"Yes, Boss," he groaned, coming around the desk.

I pushed my chair back and watched as he fell to his knees, his fangs making my cock twitch. I slowly started to undo my belt buckle, enjoying the way he swallowed at the sound of the metal clinking. I pulled it free, the leather sliding against the cloth of my pants. I stood up, looping the belt with my hands to create a collar.

"What's your safeword, Calen?" I asked, holding his needy gaze.

His pupils swelled with lust, turning his golden eyes almost onyx. "Red, Boss," he whispered hoarsely. "If I can't speak, I'll make this symbol with my hand," he said, holding up three fingers.

"No one will interrupt us this time," I whispered. "Even if you want her to."

"I kind of do," he whispered, his eyes never leaving mine.

There was a little crackle of jealousy from me, the air rippling with a little burst of energy.

"I'm still on my knees in front of *you*," Calen reminded me, licking his lips.

"Indeed," I growled, looping the belt around his neck. I tightened it just enough to give me some grip over him, but not enough to actually harm him. "Let my cock free, Calen, and I might let you swallow."

"Yes, Boss," he whispered, the tip of his claws dragging up my thighs.

The sensation made my blood burn, even though there was a layer of fabric between his nails and my skin. I bit my lower lip, my head tilting back.

Fuck. I had to stop thinking about our interruption this morning. I couldn't stop thinking about her smirk as she watched me fuck Calen.

Calen unbuttoned my pants, pulling down the zipper. I sucked in a breath as my cock sprang free, his hands gripping my hard shaft.

Some witches were more monstrous than others— and I couldn't complain that my cock reflected that part of me. I looked down, enjoying the gleam of wickedness on Calen's face as he swiped his tongue over the tip. My cock was bright blue, with veins of orange and ridges down the shaft. My cum could make my partner's body tingle all day if I wanted, and I most certainly would with Calen.

We'd been doing this for over a month now, and fuck it. I wanted to fucking breed his throat raw, and then I wanted him to remember me all day, every swallow a reminder that he was mine.

Fuck.

Calen groaned, taking the first three inches into his mouth and then his throat. The sounds he made, the way he was kneeling in front of me...

"*Calen,*" I groaned, thrusting my hips forward.

He moaned as I hit the back of his throat, and I tightened my grip on the belt around his neck, giving it a little tug.

His hands fell to my thighs, and he gripped them as I started to fuck him, not waiting. If we had the time to truly savor this, I wouldn't be so eager, but I needed to fill his mouth *before* that meeting.

I gripped his black hair with my other hand and held him still. He groaned, his body straining against me— and I made sure he wasn't using his signal.

He wasn't. He fucking loved this as much as I did.

Fuck, I was going to cum too fast. I slammed into him harder, a growl rippling through me. I could feel our magic bleeding together, the energy in the room becoming stronger and stronger. It was like listening to music, the instruments rising and rising until finally—

"FUCK," I growled, giving one last slam into his mouth.

Ropes of hot cum filled his throat, and I felt him swallow, his little groans becoming softer and longer as I filled him.

"Good boy," I whispered hoarsely, my muscles relaxing.

I pulled my cock free, tipping his face up so I could watch him lick his lips. He let out a little moan, his eyes glazed over with lust.

"Fuck, my whole body is tingling," he whispered.

"Good," I said, smiling at him. I leaned down, brushing my lips across his. Our tongues met, the taste of our magic and my cum creating a delicious combination.

He pulled back, letting out a little pant. "It's time for that meeting."

I nodded, freeing his neck from my belt. I buttoned my pants, zipped them, tucked my dress shirt, and put my belt back on.

Calen stood up, combing his fingers through his hair and pulling his glamor back on. Then, with a flick of his hand, the spell we'd put up to keep anyone from hearing us disappeared, and the door unlocked.

I sat back down in my chair just as the notification to join the meeting went off, and I pulled up the website, tapping on the join call button.

I was presented with several faces on the screen, some that I knew and some that I didn't.

In fact, some of them were monsters.

In fact, one of them belonged to none other than...

Inferna.

I fought the urge to scowl. Alex Borage, the head of the company that I worked for, cleared his throat.

"Welcome, everyone. Hope your Monday is going well. I'd like to formally welcome the head of the company known as Claws, an organization that works on some of the same products as we do," Alex said.

I could see the vein ticking in his head, and I didn't like that.

"This is a formal announcement, one that we have been

looking forward to for a while. As of this morning, Claws Inc. and Warts Inc. have become one company. We are excited to announce that we are merging to become Warts and Claws Inc. Effective immediately, we will be working together in order to roll out new collaborations that will bring the world of humans, monsters, and witches more apps and opportunities." Alex said.

I felt my soul slowly leaving my body.

A lot of smiling faces and every single one of them was a fucking mask.

This was a nightmare.

I watched one of the little hand signals fly up on Inferna's box, but she was ignored.

Alex's equivalent on the monster side, Claude— who was an ancient crusty ass vampire— cleared his throat. "I know that this will be a shock to many of you, but I expect each and every one of you to make this change with grace and excitement. Alex and I are thrilled that our companies are becoming one. The history between creatures and witches is in the past. We are all in the same world and will work together going forward. Inferna and Arthur— this merger will also immediately affect your offices. In order to ensure that there is proper collaboration, your two offices will be sharing the same floor of the building you are in. Tonight, we will have some movers coming in and setting everything up. You will be on floor nine now and will share the cafeteria floor on six. Additionally, we are excited to announce that we are installing an espresso machine for employees."

Inferna's mic was unmuted, and I could hear the venom in her voice. "With all due respect, sir, I think that it would be far more beneficial for us to keep our own floors. This is a lot of change to roll out to our teams."

"I hear you, Inferna, but this is not negotiable," Claude said, "To help with the transition, we will have our HR department on standby. Your rep, Alice, will be joining your office tomorrow."

Inferna muted herself, but I could still feel her rage bleeding through the ceiling.

I wasn't happy either. This was a fucking nightmare.

I looked up, remembering that Calen was here as well. He looked significantly less horrified than me.

"Get that smirk off your face," I hissed at him.

He snorted, shrugging. "Doesn't bother me, Boss."

"If you have any immediate concerns, please reach out to either Claude or me," Alex said, grinning. "Also, congrats, everyone. This will be huge. Thanks for joining. Have a fangtastic Monday."

A fang-fucking-tastic Monday.

CHAPTER THREE
floor 1

CALEN

Noon rolled around and I slipped into the elevator, ready for lunch. There was a little cafe down the street that I preferred to go to— mostly because they were quiet and I didn't have to deal with any witches or monsters.

I always timed it to where I would be the only one in the elevator, but instead of going down like it was supposed to, it started to lift up.

"What the fuck," I muttered, jamming the floor one button again.

No dice.

Fucking hell. I didn't want to be in an elevator with anyone. Today had already been insane, between Art breeding my fucking throat to him losing his mind after the company announcement, not to mention the bitchy side-eye I kept getting from Sally.

Everyone knew that there was something between Art

and me, but no one dared to say a damn thing. I preferred it that way.

The elevator slowed and the doors slid open, presenting me with none other than Inferna.

She stared at me for a moment, raising a dark brow. Her crimson skin was smooth and she smelled like heaven. Her black eyes glinted with a hint of mischief and she stepped into the elevator, turning around to face the door.

My eyes slid down to her ass, to her tail. Her tail had a heart-shaped tip, and then every few inches, there were knots.

As soon as the doors slid closed, a little noise left me.

"Are you still scared of me?" she asked, checking her sharp nails. "Or upset with me?"

"I'm not scared of you," I said, swallowing hard. "Or upset with you."

Fuck, my cock was hard.

She turned, studying me over her shoulder. Her dark eyes searched me, falling down to the growing bulge in my pants.

"I can see through your glamor, and I like how you look. Why do you hide yourself?" Inferna asked. "Also, please press the floor button. It's on your side of the elevator."

"Okay," I whispered, immediately lurching forward to hit the floor one button. It lit up, but the elevator didn't move.

"Hmmm," Inferna frowned. "Are you using magic to hold us here?"

"No," I wheezed. "No. Honestly, I wasn't even supposed to come to this floor, it just did it by itself."

"That's strange," she said. "Hit the button again."

I did as she said, tapping it a few times until we received a long buzz.

"Well, now it's broken. Can you fix it with magic?"

"I can't fix everything with magic," I sighed. "That's not how magic works."

"Really?" Inferna asked. "Well, I guess we'll find out soon enough."

I pressed my lips together, hunching my shoulders. "I don't hate monsters, just so you know," I whispered, "I've dated monsters and it's always been fun."

"I don't have anything inherently against witches, only ones that steal my fucking coffee pot at eight in the morning. And ones that are too busy fucking their employees instead of working. Oh, and I do not like Sally," Inferna said, crossing her arms.

We were looking at each other now. Her hair was very dark brown and fell in soft curls, her black horns stretching above her head. She was taller than me in her heels, a solid six feet, five inches of sexy monster boss energy.

"We're stuck here at least for a few minutes while this thing sorts itself out," Inferna said, her lips drawing back in a small smirk. "What's your name?"

"Calen," I said. "Not as interesting as yours."

"Inferna?" she asked, smiling even more.

Her smile could turn me into putty.

Hell, this office was dangerous. How could I be as attracted to her as I was to Art? Both were bossy and temperamental and...

"My dads did a good job of picking it out," she said, cocking her head. "I can smell your need, and I can smell *him* on you too."

"I'm not normally this horny," I whispered, "I don't know what's gotten into me."

"I'm a succubus," she said, shrugging.

"This is different," I mumbled, my cheeks heating up. I looked away from her, unsure of what else to say.

It *was* different. There was something magnetic about her. Ever since she had broken into Art's office while his cock was buried inside of me, I'd been unable to stop thinking about her.

The reason I had run away was that I didn't know why I felt the way I did right now. It was making my life hell today.

"Maybe you're going into heat," she said. "I've heard that can happen to witches."

"No, that's impossible," I whispered, even though there was a searing stab that went through my whole body. "No. That only happens if..."

Inferna's eyes flickered and she moved forward, pushing me against the elevator wall. I made a noise, my cock now fully hard and pressed against her.

She pinned her hands to either side of my head, leaning down.

"Sorry," she murmured. "But this will be the easiest way to find out, witchling."

I gasped as our lips met. I found myself unraveling at her touch, at her taste. I felt the heat inside of me unfurl, my glamor falling away. I moaned, leaning into her.

No, this *was* different.

I leaned up, winding my arms around her neck as she pressed her knee between my thighs and against my cock. My blood was singing now, my muscles burning and burning...

Fuck, I felt like I was on fire.

Our lips broke apart and I found myself kissing my way down her neck and then burying my face against her silk shirt. I breathed in her scent, letting out a moan.

"I think we might be in trouble, witchling," she whispered.

"What is happening to me?" I mumbled, breathing her scent in gasps.

I wished that Art were here too.

"Do witches have omegas?" she asked. "It's something I've seen with certain creatures, but not all."

"Sometimes," I whispered. "Especially the more monstrous ones like me."

"A little witchling omega," she murmured. "Interesting."

Inferna made a soft, feminine growl and then drew back, her expression one of pure hunger. Her red tail flicked behind her, her muscles tensing as the elevator suddenly lurched.

She took a step back, studying me like I was an alien.

"What are you doing after work?" she asked.

"I...I don't know."

"You will come up to my office at 6pm and wait for me," she said, lifting her head up. "You will need to brush your teeth prior so that I don't taste his cum, as flavorful as it is. Understood, witchling?"

"Yes," I whispered. I was trembling now, my entire body wilting in her presence.

"You can call me Mistress in private. We'll figure out what this is after work. I have to go call someone and...take care of some business. Oh, and Calen?" she said as the elevator stopped on the first floor. "You might want to put up a spell to clean up the precum spot on your pants and to mask your scent. You smell like a little omega, and quite frankly— every monster on this block is going to want to fuck you like that. Clean yourself up."

"Yes...yes, Mistress," I whispered, speechless.

What the fuck else was I supposed to say?

"Good boy," she purred, her tail flicking again.

The doors slid open and she squared her shoulders, walking out of the elevator like she was the queen of the world. Her heels clicked as she walked, her aura of power causing everyone to part and then to watch her pass in awe.

I watched her leave and then stumbled out of the elevator, my heart pounding a little faster now that she was gone.

I didn't want her to go, I realized.

Fuck. What the fuck was this?

Other people moved around the first floor, giving me side glances that made me remember what Inferna had said.

With the twist of my tongue, I whispered an incantation. My glamor intensified, protecting me from prying eyes.

I was hungry now, but for something very very different from when I had initially stepped foot in the elevator.

How the hell was I supposed to eat lunch when I wanted to eat Infera's pussy?

I waved my badge over the little gate, heading out into the lobby and then out the swinging front door. It was August and the air was finally starting to cool down in our city. I took a deep breath, trying to shake myself of the feeling of lust.

Between Inferna and Art, I was a fucking goner today. My head wasn't clear and I couldn't... think of anything except both of them fucking me. Both of them taking me.

Should I tell Art about Inferna wanting to see me?

We weren't dating. We hadn't seen each other outside of work at all. It was just that, some mornings I found his cock in my ass and our cum all over his desk.

I headed down the sidewalk, focusing on the hum of the

city. I headed to the cafe, slipping inside the quiet space and inhaling the scent of fresh bread. I ordered my food and coffee and then found a window seat.

I only had an hour, well...now, thirty minutes to try and figure out if I was actually going to do as Inferna had told me.

I had to decide if I was going to tell Art.

He had never shared anything personal with me. For all I knew, he could actually be married. He could have twelve kids and counting with a dog and house and—

The waitress set my food and coffee down, giving me a familiar smile, and then leaving. I took a bite of my sandwich and regretfully, could barely taste it now that all I could think about was Inferna and Art.

My blood was still humming from swallowing his cum too, the magic of it settling in. It was making me feel like I was running a fucking fever.

All I could think about was being tag teamed by those two, trading tail for cock over and over again until I couldn't cum anymore. As much as I loved being dominated by Art, I wanted to see just how submissive he'd be beneath Inferna.

There was no way he would be able to go against her. Not in that way.

I simply loved submission, which was why I gave in to him. I loved the way it felt to give, to allow someone else to take over for a bit. And with the right person, the trust I felt in giving my submission to a partner was exhilarating.

I wished I could give myself fully to Art, but he wouldn't give himself to me. But maybe with Inferna...

I polished off my food, drained my coffee, took my plates to the front, and then hit the sidewalk again.

As I made my way inside the office building and then headed up to my floor, I made my decision.

When Inferna got off work today, I would be waiting for her.

If Art really wanted me, then we would talk about it. But, until then, I planned on letting the stunning succubus take me however she pleased.

My cock twitched, my body burning all over again.

Just the thought alone of waiting for her put hellfire in my bones.

I wanted to hear her call me a good boy again.

I wanted to taste her sweet mouth again, to let her forked tongue...

I shivered. I'd forgotten about her tongue until now.

"Hey man, you need to press the floor button so the elevator can go up."

I looked up, startled out of my thoughts. Two strangers were waiting patiently.

"Right, sorry," I breathed, hitting the buttons.

Fucking hell, making it to the end of the day was going to be torture.

CHAPTER FOUR
end of day espionage

INFERNA

I called my Uncle Dell on my lunch break and found out that I could not hire a hitman for the CEO of the Warts Company— and that I could not hire a hitman for Arthur either.

Not only had I been given a lesson on how that was an inappropriate solution to a problem, but I was also reminded that monsters don't kill witches anymore and that we tried very hard to be respectable members of society.

I should have called Rum. Uncle Rum would have handed over Uncle B's secret list, somehow.

Fucking hell, today had turned into a shit show.

Not to mention, the elevator...

Calen was mine, that I was sure of.

"Boss?" Poppins asked, stealing my attention back to the conversation at hand.

Everyone was waiting for me to speak. I let out a little sigh, rolling my shoulders.

"This sounds like bad news," Stripes growled, his tiger face scrunching in annoyance.

"Well, it depends on how you view it," I said. "This morning, I had a conference call with the company. We are being merged with Warts Inc., and the new company name will be Warts & Claws Inc. They are also forcing us to share a floor with the witches in order to encourage collaboration, as well as dropping an HR representative on our doorstep like a fucking present."

Everyone stared at me for a moment, and then everything erupted. One of the demons started hissing with his seven tongues, his nine eyes burning with rage. One of the wolf boys started cussing up a storm with Poppins. Loralie, a pixie demon girl with piercings and black eyes, started singing a song about raining hell down on our enemies.

"EVERYONE QUIET!" I bellowed, my voice snapping everyone out of their rage. I crossed my arms, glaring around the room. "I'm not happy about this either, but monsters and witches have been together for a long time. The only reason we don't have witches in this office is that none have applied. They're just as much creature as we are."

"It's not that they're witches," Loralie chimed, "It's *those* witches. The ones in that office. They have bad vibes."

Everyone agreed, mumbling their opinions.

I staved off a groan, grinding my teeth.

"This is no different than working with humans," Poppins said.

"And?" I asked. "That's what we want. The more widely known monsters become in the human world, the better it is to actually be around them. And witches aren't humans. A lot of the problems in this area seem to stem from some of the things that happened years ago between one coven and monsters. But that's in the past and has nothing to do with us now."

"Witches are just like vampires," one of them growled.

"Vampires, witches, monsters, humans," I said. "I don't give a fuck what you are so long as you behave and treat all with respect. Tomorrow, we will start working on floor nine. Also, apparently, they're getting us an espresso machine."

I only got one whoop from that, and it was half-hearted at best.

"Alright," I said, glancing at the clock on the wall. "It's almost 6 p.m. Everyone, you're good to go for the evening. Thank you for having another successful day, we knocked out a shit ton of tasks."

Perhaps it was a bit manipulative, but I really pushed on the last compliment. I watched everyone preen under my words, their worries soothed. Everyone got up to leave, chatting amongst themselves.

Everyone but Poppins.

Poppins was a good friend, had been for years. We'd met our freshman year in college and stuck to each other since then. He arched a feathered brow.

"What?" I hissed.

He snorted. "Do you really think this is a good idea?"

I threw my hands up, "What other choice do we have? I fought it. I'll keep fighting it. But they made their choice. We're simply going to have to deal with it."

Poppins sighed, his tawny feathers ruffling a little. He smoothed them out and then rose from his seat, even taller than me. His wings spread out some, his muscles rippling beneath his coat as he crossed his arms.

"Also, you smell like you devoured someone," he said.

"Yes, and I need you to leave because I'm meeting someone," I hissed quietly.

"And no details?!" he scoffed.

I started to herd him towards the front of the office, to the elevators. "I'll tell you everything once we make it to our Friday drinks. I'm not saying shit until then."

"But so much can happen!" Poppins complained.

"Yes, I know," I said, "Get out, Poppins."

I jabbed the elevator button for my friend, ignoring his little pout as I all but shoved him in once the doors opened. He gave me a thumbs-up as they shut and I turned, feeling the shimmer of magic now that I was alone.

If witches could appear in places, then I wasn't sure why they used things like elevators. Still, I was pleased to see Calen waiting for me once I walked back into the office, standing outside my door.

He met my gaze and I felt it again— a low, heated thrum in my stomach. An ache, a need. Lust and desire.

I'd been so fucking focused on rescuing my coffee machine this morning that I hadn't paid attention to the way I had felt when seeing him. But now that I had touched him, now that I had kissed him...

I crossed the room to him, enjoying the way he sucked in his breath. He let his glamor fall, and even beneath the emerald color of his skin, I could see the light flush.

Fuck, he smelled like sin.

"Art is going to be mad at me," he whispered.

I raised a brow, stopping in front of him. "Are you two exclusive? Because if that is the case, then we won't continue."

"No," Calen said, shaking his head. "No. Neither of us has said that. But also, I don't think either one of us wants just one partner."

I hummed, thinking about his answer. "You should perhaps talk to him if it's going to make you anxious. I wasn't planning on devouring you quite yet, anyway. I'm a bit classier than that. I was going to make you cum and then steal you off for dinner."

"Oh," he said, his eyes widening. "Fuck. I haven't cum today."

"Awww," I purred, leaning down to brush my lips over his forehead. "My witchling is thirsty, hmm?"

"Yes, Mistress," he huffed.

His scent immediately spiked, the aroma of sandalwood and jasmine becoming spicier as his heat rose.

He was definitely in heat, too. He was not just a normal witch, and he was most certainly going to be mine.

I had woken up this morning not thinking anything about taking on a mate. In fact, I truly enjoyed my freedom. I liked being single and then occasionally taking a partner to feed— but it was never more than that. Even when I went to clubs or parties, it was never more than just that.

But this... this would be different. I knew what happened when a monster found their mate. I knew about my dads, and about the rest of my family. Aunt Penny and Aunt Kat had told me more and more details as I had gotten older.

The only difference was, that had been their experience as humans.

Only Luna and Naomi, who were also in our family, had been the ones to truly be able to help me once I'd started to *hunger* for more. I was lucky to have the big family I did— and one that was a mix of crazy monsters and humans.

Still, I was self-aware enough to recognize that I not only wanted Calen— I wanted to own his body, soul, and mind. I wanted him to be *mine*.

Arthur was a different story. I was still too pissed over having to share an office with that fucking bossy twat.

Still, the two of them were connected.

I tipped up Calen's chin with a claw, holding his honeyed gaze. "Sweet boy," I murmured. "What would you like right now?"

"He needs both of us."

I looked up, surprised to see Arthur stepping through a bright blue circle. His eyes were the same color, and seared the same way that lighting did a stormy sky.

"What the fuck do you want? We don't need to see each other until tomorrow," I hissed.

"I realized earlier why I was so desperate for you," Arthur said, looking directly at Calen and ignoring me. "And then after lunch, I saw her on you. Her aura," he growled, looking at me. "And then I noticed that you stayed after work. Then you came up here. Now, I've found you in the arms of our fucking corporate enemy. This is espionage."

I snorted, amused and slightly offended.

"She's not my enemy," Calen said, his voice losing the soft edge he had when he was with me. "I told you earlier that I liked how I felt when she was watching."

This was starting to get a lot stickier than I had planned, not to mention that I legitimately had called my uncle earlier asking him to find me a hitman for the blue-eyed witchy boss.

"I think the witchling is in heat," I said, looking at Arthur.

He opened his mouth to speak but then stopped, scowling. "That's somewhat rare in our world."

"I know," I said, "But I can smell it. I can smell how needy he is. Maybe it's because I'm a succubus, maybe it's because he belongs to me, but I am certain he is going into it. He will need to be cared for."

"Fuck," Arthur said. "That does change things. And what do you mean *yours?*"

"He is mine," I said, glaring at Arthur. "If you want to fight for him, I will. I wanted to kill you earlier. Turns out we're not supposed to hire hitmen."

"I wasn't thinking very kind things about you either. Still not. Calen is mine," Arthur growled.

"You sound so cute when you try to growl," I said, lunging across the room for him.

I ignored Calen's gasp of surprise as I shoved Arthur against a desk, my tail wrapping around his wrists and pinning them above his head against the top before he could fight me. He let out another pitiful growl and I hissed, silencing him.

"I could burn you with my magic," he snarled.

"Can both of you be nice?!" Calen cried.

"No!" We both barked.

Arthur twisted in my grip and I felt the magic hit me, shoving me back. I caught myself before one of my heels snapped, now truly feeling the monster inside me awaken.

Calen stepped in front of me, his eyes pleading. "Please stop. Please! Please, both of you. I can't handle this right now. I literally feel like I'm running a fever."

I bared my fangs, my chest heaving with angry breaths. I wanted to choke Arthur to death and watch the life drain from his pretty blue—

"Inferna," Calen moaned. "Please."

I felt his hand slide over my waist and I watched in satisfaction as Arthur glared.

"I don't know what's happening," Calen groaned.

"You," I said, looking down at him, "are about to be in a

fucking heat that will only be broken by sex. And naturally, being a succubus, it is affecting me greatly. Not to mention that Mr. Snake-up-his-ass is obviously feeling the same effects that I am, despite not being able to smell your scent like I can."

"At this point, call me Art," he growled, glaring.

"Art," I snipped. "Arthur. The bane of my fucking existence since eight this morning. What happened to the suave man that composed himself earlier?"

"He went home early," Art snarled. "Give me Calen. I will take care of him."

"Absolutely not," I sneered. "He is mine. I will take him to my home and fuck him until his heat breaks, and then figure out everything else after. He belongs to me."

"I had him first."

"Well, it's a good thing he's not a toy," I growled. "Otherwise, I would have to break your neck."

"I want both of you," Calen whimpered.

We both looked at him, caught off guard by his tone.

Fuck, he was needy. His cheeks were flushed, his cock hard and creating an outline in his pants. He was now standing between Arthur and me, his scent making even Art groan.

"Fuck," Art whispered. "Fucking hell. What the fuck is this?"

"Chaos," I mumbled, swallowing hard.

It was difficult to think about how angry Art made me when a needy little witchling was aching for me. My stomach gave a slow tug, my body craving him. I could feel the sharpness of my teeth, the need to taste his blood and mate him becoming harder and harder to ignore.

I had just met him this morning. It was a fucking Monday too.

Art took a step closer, his expression softening. For a moment, I could see what Calen saw in him. The gentle charm, the sweetness.

"Calen," he said softly. "I'm sorry I didn't realize that you were in heat."

"I've never been," he rasped, swallowing hard. "I didn't feel anything until this morning and then throughout the day it's gotten worse and worse."

"Hmm," Art frowned, stealing a glance at me. "Maybe you set it off?"

"It might have been your cum," I said, thinking about the lingering taste I'd savored when kissing Calen.

Art flushed, his jaw stiffening for a moment. "Fuck. Maybe. I've never...I've never done that to you," he said. "I have to intentionally give that, and then it stays with you all day."

"Whatever," Calen said, his voice almost hoarse. "Fuck. I'm a mess. I don't know what to do."

I mulled it over for a moment, deciding if I was going to cave.

Was I going to let Art join Calen and me?

Wouldn't it be irresponsible if I didn't?

"My apartment is around the corner," I said. "We can go to my place. Tomorrow is a big day for all of us, and hopefully, we can sate you enough to not throw everything off..."

"We can try..." Art drifted off, scowling. "I can leave after."

I arched a brow. "He will need us all night, *witch*."

Art made a strangled noise, looking away. "I won't stay the night."

Calen whimpered and I moved closer to him, my tail

moving around and winding around his hips. He gave a little thrust, his expression one of absolute need.

"So needy," I murmured. "You don't have to stay the night," I said, looking at Art. "I can stay with him."

Art's shoulders stiffened and then he gave a nod, moving closer. "I can transport us to your apartment if you give me the location and a strand of your hair."

I fought the urge to laugh, because at this point— it really wasn't a laughing matter. Every moment that I wasn't fucking Calen was another moment of torture for both of us.

"Fine," I said, reaching up and pulling one free. I gave it to Art, watching as he made a signal and it caught on fire. "Try not to portal us to hell. But my address is 8101 Dragon Lane, apartment 810."

Art nodded and took a step back. He drew a circle with his finger, and the floor was matched— an electric blue circle drawn around the three of us.

Fucking hell, I had really just invited two witches over to my home.

Art stepped up to us again, this time tugging Calen between the two of us. Our little witchling groaned, his head tilting back. "Please," he rasped.

Art growled, shaking his head. "I can't believe I'm doing this. Alright, here we go."

With a thrumming whoosh, we were sucked into his portal— landing in my apartment on the other side.

CHAPTER FIVE
submission to a succubus

ART

I had planned on fighting Inferna tooth and nail, not fucking Calen with her. I had also planned on confronting her at the office, when I realized that he was acting strange.

Then I'd started putting things together.

I wasn't an idiot. I'd made it as far as I had because I was good at figuring things out. I *was* good at leading when I wasn't filling up Calen...

The three of us landed in Inferna's apartment, and it wasn't what I had expected. I had expected sleek lines and dark furniture, modern and cold.

Instead, her apartment looked like someone had let a paint pallet explode. It was pleasant, in a way. Homey.

Maybe I was misjudging her.

Calen groaned, pressing his ass back against my already hard cock. I let out a breath, sliding my hands down his sides and gripping his hips.

Inferna's tail was still wrapped around Calen and she didn't hesitate to lean down and kiss him.

Fuck. *Fuck.*

She *devoured* him. She was the sexiest monster I'd ever met in my life and watching her kiss him, her black nails gripping his hair and pulling his head back...

Her black eyes met mine and I felt the urge to succumb. To do whatever the hell she wanted me to.

I liked dominating. I liked being in control.

But...

She broke their kiss despite Calen's whine, her tongue running over her crimson lips. "We need to talk about boundaries before we go any further."

"My safeword is red," Calen rasped. "And if I need you to slow down then I will say yellow. If I can't speak, then I'll make a signal like this," he said, showing his hand.

Inferna nodded, pleased at his response.

Fuck, the way she set boundaries and rules was beyond sexy.

"And you?" Inferna asked.

"I don't really need one," I mumbled.

"Then you can sit on the couch and watch. I won't play with you if you won't be safe, and I won't let you touch Calen either."

I parted my lips and then closed them. She was right. And it was stupid of me to resist.

"Red, yellow, and green works for me too," I said, swallowing hard.

"Excellent," she said, smiling. "We will use that then. I'm going to eat the two of you up," she said, tipping up Calen's chin.

He whimpered and I knew he was hard. *I* was hard.

"I know that you like to lead," Inferna said, "but you

will obey me in my space. Both of you will. Do you understand?"

Every second that passed, I felt my will crumbling. Inferna was focused on me now, Calen already hers completely.

"I'll still let you fuck him how you want," Inferna said. "But it does mean that if I tell you to wait to cum, and you disobey, that you will be punished."

My breath left me and I swallowed hard.

Fuck it. I was always the one in control. I never gave in to others and every fucking moment of my life, I was always the one to act. To control. To make plans.

Giving in for a little while...

Maybe it wouldn't be too bad.

"Fine," I huffed. "Fine. Fuck. I want you although I don't like you."

"Likewise," she mused, smirking. "But I'll forget about that for a little while."

"Please," Calen whimpered.

"Shhh," she hummed, giving him a soft pet, "I'm going to make you feel better, witchling," she said, her voice making me want to drool. The tone she had was pure sex, her words melting the last bit of my restraint. "Are you going to be good boys?" she asked.

"Yes," I breathed, surprising even myself.

Inferna smiled, her tail unwinding from Calen as she drew him in for a kiss. I watched the tip of her tail reach out, brushing over the front of my dress pants.

I groaned, my head tipping back. Her touch alone was enough to set my blood on fire, filling me with need.

"Take off your clothes," she purred. "Both of you can strip the other."

"Yes, Mistress," Calen whispered.

I raised a brow, my breath catching as her eyes fell on me. "Yes, Mistress," I whispered hoarsely, surprised at how good it felt to address her as such.

"Mmm, a good little switch," she said, her tail running over my belt buckle. "Strip our witchling and then he can unclothe you, understood?"

"Yes," I said, this time obeying.

Calen turned and looked at me, his glamor completely falling away now. I loved him in this form, a primal witch state that I might have envied a little. He was beautiful.

He leaned up, our lips meeting in a hungry kiss.

I never kissed him enough. I never spent enough time truly savoring his presence.

Fuck. I could have done things differently, but I hadn't.

I raked my nails down Calen's back and then moved to his front, running them over his hard muscled chest. I started with the top button of his shirt as we kissed, our tongues fighting for dominance as I began to strip him.

I pulled his shirt free and then pulled off the undershirt, pausing to look down at him.

Fuck, I'd never actually seen him completely naked.

His eyes lit up. "What is it?"

"You're hot," I whispered. "Hot and mine. Fuck, I can't believe I never took you home, Calen."

His gaze flickered and he made a noise. "I never thought you wanted to."

"I've thought about it many times, I've just always been so rushed," I admitted. "I'll make up for it, I promise."

Inferna made a hum of approval and I felt her move behind me. My muscles tensed as I felt her nails run down my own spine.

"Oh hell," I whispered, swallowing hard.

"Get his clothes off, Art," she whispered.

Calen moaned as I leaned down, unbuckling his pants and sliding them, along with his boxers, to the floor. His cock sprang free, hard and aching with need. It was dark green and covered with scales just like the rest of his body, dark ridges pulsing with his magic.

My magic primarily came out bright blue, while his was golden. Every time he did a spell or used his magic, I'd see the little whisps and sparkles of gold.

That same magic could turn inward, enhancing one's body during sex in fun ways. For him, it meant that he would cum *a lot*.

I planned on licking up every single drop. I swiped the tip with my thumb and then turned, offering it to Inferna.

"Truce," I murmured. "Please."

Her dark eyes lit up with delight and she leaned forward, sucking it clean. I shivered, longing to feel her lips around my cock. "I accept fully," she said. "Witchling, strip him for us."

Calen moaned and then began to free me of my clothes, tossing them to the floor. We were standing in Inferna's living room and her couch was large enough for the three of us to do a lot of fun things with each other.

Inferna's lips brushed over the curve of my neck while Calen's hand wrapped around my cock. I groaned, tipping my head back.

"You make such good noises," Inferna praised. "I want you to suck Calen's cock. I think he deserves the attention, don't you?"

"Yes," I rasped, an involuntary groan leaving me as she nipped my neck.

She was careful not to actually break the skin, careful not to draw blood with her sharp fangs. Her hand slid up to my shoulder and then she gave me a light shove, pushing me towards the ground.

I fell to my knees in front of them, looking up as they leaned in to kiss each other.

"You're still clothed," I said to Inferna.

She smiled, "I'll undress when I please. Suck our omega's cock, witch."

"Yes, Mistress," I said.

I focused on Calen's cock and leaned forward, swirling my tongue over the tip. He groaned, his hips thrusting a little. He was so needy, his skin hot to the touch. All I wanted to do right now was make him cum over and over again until he couldn't stop.

I'd never met an omega witch before and now all I could think about was how he was mine.

I'd had countless failed relationships and a lot of issues that had come from them, but this...this felt different.

Everything about this was different.

Inferna gave my head a light shove and I groaned as I swallowed his shaft, taking him down my throat. I began to suck him, moving my head back and forth as I drove him wild.

"Fuck!" he cried, making little noises as he began to fuck my throat harder. "Fuck. I can't get enough, I need you," he moaned.

"You have him, witchling," Inferna hummed. "He's sucking your cock so well," she whispered. "Servicing you like you deserve. Do you like how his mouth feels on your hard cock?"

"Yes, Mistress," he moaned. "I love it. It feels *so good*," he panted.

"Good boy," she whispered, "He's such a good little slut sucking your cock, hmmm?"

Fuck. I closed my eyes for a moment, reveling in her calling me a slut. I liked the way it made me feel, enjoying just how fucking wild it was driving me already.

She leaned down, her lips brushing across my ear. "I can smell your arousal, can taste just how fucking hard you are right now. Your scent changes when I say something you like," she chuckled. "And I now know you like being called a slut. Isn't that right?"

I drew back from Calen's cock for a moment, panting. "Yes. Fucking hell, you drive me crazy."

She reached around and gripped my jaw, pushing my head forward so that I would keep sucking Calen's cock. I grunted as he hit the back of my throat, helpless between the two of them.

"I didn't tell you to stop," she purred. "I want to hear you choke on him, Art. I want you to drink his cum like it's the last thing you'll ever taste."

I groaned, my cock pulsing against my thigh. Inferna knelt behind me as Calen continued to fuck me, his movements becoming wilder and wilder. I was driving him crazy, dragging him straight to the edge of pleasure.

I wanted to please him. I wanted to make him cum. He was mine and his heat... this feeling...

The tip of Inferna's tail brushed over my skin, dragging lightly as it came around to my cock.

I moaned, my vision blurring for a second as a fierce wave hit me.

What Calen had said earlier rang true— this *was* different.

Calen gripped my hair now and I felt him, how close he was to the edge. I wanted to feel him more, though, craving a bond much deeper and much more serious than anything I'd ever made with anyone.

The spell was at the front of my mind now but I chased it away, opening my eyes just as Calen lost himself completely. He cried out, his muscles tensing as he started to cum. The taste of him filled my mouth and I swallowed, savoring everything.

Inferna's hand reached around me now, pumping my shaft as I kept swallowing Calen's seed. I groaned as he pulled free, noting that he was still hard and dripping.

"Calen," I groaned. "Fuck, you're still dripping."

"He will be until we break the heat," Inferna said. "It could take days."

"Days?" Calen and I both rasped.

"Indeed. We'll figure it out. Calen, go to the couch and bend over. I want you to wait while I play with Art," Inferna commanded.

"Okay," Calen said, biting his bottom lip. His eyes lingered on us for a few moments and then he went to the couch, bending over for us.

I had a perfect view of his ass, of his still hard cock waiting to be stroked all over again.

Inferna gripped my jaw, forcing me to keep my eyes on Calen. "I want you to remember that you obey me. Do you understand?"

"Yes, Mistress," I whined. "I swear, I will listen to you."

"Even if Calen begs you to keep going— if I tell you to stop, you listen."

"Yes, Mistress."

"If I tell you to fill him up with cum, you listen."

"Yes, Mistress."

"Good little slut," she said. "Remember your safeword."

"Yes, Mistress," I whined. "Please let me fuck him. My cock is aching for him."

"Not yet," she said. "I'm going to play with him first. I

want you to sit here and watch. You aren't allowed to touch your own cock. Do you understand?"

"Yes," I said, biting my bottom lip.

"Good boy," she praised. "Now, you can watch how your Mistress makes our little witchling cum."

CHAPTER SIX
knotty boys

CALEN

My entire body felt like it had been thrown into a cauldron. I felt like I drank four different potions and then added alcohol on top of it, every muscle and bone in my body aching with potent lust.

I couldn't stop. I couldn't stop myself from crying out with every little touch. My cock didn't even belong to me anymore, it belonged to my monstrous Mistress.

I was hers. I was Art's. I couldn't think about work, about the office, or about anything unless it was the two of them.

Inferna stepped up behind me and I looked down, between my legs and past my cock. I could see the shape of her and I watched as she began to slowly slip off her clothing.

Fuck. I could cum from just watching her strip.

Fuck. I *was going to cum* from just watching her strip.

"Let it out, baby," she breathed. "Watch me strip for

you. I can taste how hot you think I am. Admittedly, I'm even feeding off it."

I wanted her to feed off me. Hell, if she asked me to— I would be her own personal pet. She could fuck me and drink from me anytime she wanted.

"Little witchling," she murmured.

Fuck. My cock started to pulse and I gasped as cum spurted out, landing on her couch.

"Oh god, I'm sorry," I rasped.

"Don't be sorry," she purred. "We have someone who can lick it up. Don't be sorry again for cumming."

"Yes, Mistress," I whimpered.

Her clothing was free now and I turned my head over my shoulder, sucking in a breath.

She was glorious. Tall and lean, with beautiful breasts and...

"You have wings," I gasped.

Her black wings stretched behind her, smooth like leather.

"I do when I let my form truly relax," she said, smirking. "Wings in the office are a little harder to keep from causing trouble."

She was stunning. Her heart-shaped face tipped to the side, her fangs glistening in the amber lighting of her apartment. Her living room was full of bright colors, art decorating the walls behind her. Her couch was soft leather and perfect for me to be kneeling over.

Her tail had a mind of its own it seemed. She moved closer to me, the heat of her overwhelming me. I could feel the energy in the room as if someone had cast a spell.

Only, there was no spell.

This was the energy we all created by being with each other.

I looked past her to Art. He was kneeling, his eyes piercing the two of us as her tail brushed across my skin. I moaned, meeting his gaze.

His cock was so hard. He was so needy and he wanted me so badly, but she was making him wait.

Seeing him wait for me was enough to make me gasp, a fresh wave of pleasure overcoming me.

"My little witchling wants to be bred," she whispered.

My cock jerked, my moan filling the room.

I wanted her to breed and fuck me. Bite me and use me.

"Please," I rasped.

"Maybe I'll make Art cum on my tail and then fuck you with it, so that it's like I came inside you."

"Mistress," I moaned. "I'm not worthy of you."

She chuckled, the tip brushing over my ass. I gasped, feeling how...wet I was?

"Mm," she hummed. "You're slick like a little bitch in heat. So cute."

The tip of her tail slowly pushed into me and I gasped, digging my fingers into her couch cushion.

"Ohhh," she chuckled. "Art," she said, patting her thigh like he was a dog. "Crawl to me and then lick up the mess he's making."

I heard his breath hitch, followed by him obeying.

He never let others take over. He never let himself be submissive.

But he still crawled. He still submitted to our succubus Mistress.

Her tail pushed in further and I cried out, my head falling forward. I pressed my forehead against my forearms, giving her an even better angle to drive her tail inside of me.

I felt Art close now and looked down, watching him lick up my drops of cum.

"Good boys," Inferna chimed. "So good. Lick up everything," she commanded.

I felt his tongue swipe over my thighs, licking up any drops he could find. I cried out again as the head of her tail finally fit inside me, stretching me wider than I ever had been before.

Fuck. This was torture. Heaven and hell, sin and pleasure.

I felt his tongue swipe around my ass, pausing to lick her tail too.

Inferna and I both made noises, and it dawned on me just how sensitive her tail was.

Inferna's tail pulled free, before plunging back deep inside of me. I yelped, the feeling of being taken making my entire body react. She began to fuck me, thrusting it inside of me over and over again. All the while, Art continued to lap everything up.

He groaned, desperate for more. Desperate for relief.

"Mistress," Art whined. "Can I lick you too? You're wet..."

I looked back, groaning as I realized he was right. Our Mistress was wet, I could see her essence glistening between her thighs. She lifted her leg, planting her foot on the cushion next to me and giving Art the perfect angle to play with her.

"Lick me, then, you hungry little slut," she said.

Her tail went deeper and the two of us cried out together as Art leaned forward, devouring her. She let out a soft breath, her head tipping back with a moan.

"Mmm, I like how your tongue feels. Dripping with

magic and his cum and me," Inferna growled. "You can use your magic if you want."

Art groaned and I felt the little zap in the air, followed by her cry.

Followed by my own. I was lost in the two of them, listening to the sounds of pleasure. Her tail continued to fuck me and I felt so close to cumming, my breaths getting shorter and shorter.

Inferna yelled at the same moment I did, the two of us cumming together. Her tail pulled free and I collapsed forward, groaning. I was covered in cum and sweat and...fuck.

"I'm still hard," I whimpered.

Why was I still hard? This was torture.

"Take him to my bedroom," Inferna moaned.

I felt Art's hands run up my body and then gasped as he lifted me, holding me to his chest like a bride.

"Bed?" Art asked.

I looked, surprised to see Inferna with her eyes still shut. "Bedroom down the hall. He needs to fuck one of us."

I made a little noise, the idea of filling one of them with my hot cum making me writhe. Art grunted, his grip on me tightening.

"So needy," he crooned softly.

Inferna chuckled and then led the way. I watched her lithe body move across the apartment, admiring her ass and tail.

She led us to her bedroom, the door pushed open as we stepped inside. She turned on a light as Art carried me to her bed, lying me down.

His mouth caught mine, dragging me into a heady kiss. I groaned against him, savoring his taste.

He tasted like our Mistress' cum.

My body was going crazy again now, the feeling of need making me writhe beneath Art's muscled body. I dragged my fingers up his back, enjoying his little gasp in my mouth.

Fuck.

Inferna crawled onto the bed next to me and I was promptly pulled to the center, Art taking the other side.

How was I so lucky? The way that they touched me, kissed me...

Inferna swirled her forked tongue over one of my nipples, making me cry out. She scraped her teeth over my skin while Art continued to kiss me, his hand sliding down to my cock. Cum dripped from the tip and he swirled his thumb over the top, breaking our mouths apart so he could lick it up.

"This is crazy," I rasped, but the heat was rising all over again.

I couldn't fight it. I could only succumb to it.

Art gripped my cock and my hips thrust forward as Inferna continued to torture me. I felt her tail trail up my leg and then wind around my thigh, pulling it away from my other.

Both of them were working in tandem now. Part of me wondered if they had a telepathic link because for every nip of pain Inferna delivered, it was followed by a kiss from Art.

I was theirs. I wanted to be theirs forever.

Art groaned as I dragged my fingers through his dark hair. He slid down my body, his cock hard and ready.

"Ride him, witch," Inferna demanded, her voice sending a shiver down my spine.

Art...ride me?

My eyes widened as he straddled me, his skin gleaming

with sweat and magic. His body glowed, his eyes brighter than lightning.

His cock wasn't like a normal cock and it wasn't very often that I got to really look at it. It was bright blue with a sloped head, the same one that always managed to send me over the edge. There were small ridges up the side, and then at the base... there was a knot.

He'd never knotted me before, I realized.

Fuck, I wanted him to knot me.

Inferna hummed her approval. She turned and grabbed a bottle of lube from her side table.

"Mmm, and they say witches are closer to humans than monsters. I think I disagree. I think witches are just as monstrous as we are," she said, pouring some of the lube into her hand. She reached out and rubbed some on my cock and then his ass, getting us both ready.

Once she was satisfied we were both ready, she touched his cock. She gripped the base, stroking his vibrant knot. "This will be perfect to lock you into our witchling. And then once he fucks you, and you fuck him, it will be my turn."

Art groaned, his head tipping back. His lips parted, his jaw stiffening as he made little noises at her touch. His muscles rippled as he reached back, parting his ass as he slowly began to lower himself.

He opened his eyes, our gazes locking right as the tip of my cock spread him.

Fuck. Fuck. That look. Art had never looked at me like *this*.

"Art," I whimpered. "*Fuck*."

Inferna began to stroke his cock as he slid himself further, taking my cock inch by inch. I gasped as pure heat stabbed me, rushing through my veins. I was desperate, I realized, desperate to fuck him. To breed him. To fill him with my cum.

Fuck. Where were these thoughts coming from? I'd always wanted to be fucked. Now, I was the one wanting to do everything to him.

Inferna made a gentle noise, reaching up to cup my face. I looked at her, breathing her breath as our lips parted on a kiss. She smiled against me.

"You're so cute, little witchling. So desperate to fill him," she whispered. "Mmmm, I can taste your lust. I think I could live off it for centuries."

"Please," I rasped. "Bite me. Mate me."

Her dark eyes flickered and she cocked her head right as Art fully seated himself. His muscles throbbed around my cock and I gasped, thrusting into him.

He grunted and leaned back, his hands planting on my thighs.

Inferna gave me another little kiss and then moved her lips to my ear. "I'll mate you once you aren't crazed with this heat, little witchling. But you're still mine. You're still his."

My eyes teared up, my vision blurring as I gave another thrust. Art and I cried out together as I started to cum. Filling him up, feeling myself let go entirely, all of it was complete euphoric pleasure.

"Good boy," Inferna purred. "Fuck him, Art."

Art slowly slid off with a grunt and before I had a moment to recover, I was rolled over onto my stomach. Art straddled me again, but this time I felt the tip of his cock already pushing inside of me.

"Art," I gasped. "Fuck, please. Please breed me."

"Fuck him, Art," Inferna growled. "Hard and fast."

"Yes, Mistress," he gasped.

He thrust forward, filling me completely with his ridged cock. I gasped, gripping the blankets beneath me as he pumped into me. I pressed my nose against the bed, breathing in Inferna's scent.

This was heaven. It had to be.

Inferna moved and I lifted my head as she sat in front of me, parting her legs.

Fuck. Her pussy was perfect and unlike anything I'd seen before. Her clit was swollen with need, and I realized that her entrance was lined with...

"Teeth?" I gasped.

Art gave a hard thrust and I cried out, trying to process my thoughts.

"Mhmm," Inferna hummed. "Don't worry, they won't hurt you," she chuckled. "Lick me while he breeds you, witchling. Make your Mistress cum."

I was desperate to lick her while Art fucked me. She chuckled and moved forward and I immediately started lapping at her clit. Her nails raked through my hair and she gripped my head, shoving my mouth down.

"Don't be afraid," she teased.

Fucking hell. Art grunted as he fucked me and I found myself giving in, burying my tongue inside of her. The tips of the fangs were sharp, but it felt...

Fuck, it felt good. She tasted like heaven and I didn't care if I breathed again. I needed to devour her.

"Fuck it, I'm knotting you," Art gasped.

My whole body lit up with magic as he gave one final pump, his knot shoving inside of me. I withdrew my tongue from Inferna for a moment, crying out as he spread me. His knot pulsed inside of me, locking his body to mine. I felt his cum filling me, coming out in hot spurts.

He leaned down, his breath against my ear. "*Mine,*" he

growled. "Eat your Mistress," he demanded, giving my head a shove.

I buried my face against her pussy, sliding my tongue inside of her again. I felt the pinpricks of pain, but it was followed by wave after wave of pleasure.

I groaned, feeling Art's knot swell even more. Between the two of them, I couldn't think about anything but how good everything felt.

Art leaned forward, his face moving in with mine. Inferna gasped as he began to lick her clit while I thrust my tongue in and out of her.

"Mmm," she purred. "Such good boys."

I was determined to make her cum. Art and I devoured her and I felt his magic pick up, followed by Inferna's groan.

She was getting closer and I wanted to taste her. I needed to drink from her.

"Fuck, I'm so close," Inferna gasped.

Art and I both took that as a cue to give her everything we had. The three of us groaned together as we fucked her with our tongues, and finally— she let out a sharp cry. I felt her cum on my tongue, her muscles tightening around me as she flooded my mouth.

I felt the teeth scrape against me and groaned, licking up every drop.

"I want to taste," Art groaned.

I moved my mouth, allowing him to take my place. His knot pulsed hot inside of me as he lapped her, her pants making me hard all over again.

"Mmmm," Inferna moaned. "Now it's truly my turn."

CHAPTER SEVEN
vagina fangs

INFERNA

The first orgasm the two of them had given me had been delicious, but my entire body still hummed with need.

It would take a lot more than cumming once to truly satisfy me. I already felt high from the magic and scent of all of our lust, of the taste of Calen's heat— but I needed more.

I would lock his cock inside of me, just like Art was locked inside of him.

Art, despite us hating each other, was good in bed and he also seemed to know what I was thinking. His bright blue eyes glimmered with mischief and he wrapped his arms around Calen, rolling the two of them over.

Calen gasped, his eyes widening as his cock was hard and standing straight up. I slid off the bed and went to my dresser, pulling out a small box of body wipes. I went back to them, pulling out a couple to clean his cock.

He moaned, his head falling back next to Art's. "Please," he gasped.

Monsters were immune to STIs and STDs, but I still wanted him to be clean before I locked his cock inside of me.

"Messy boys," I murmured.

Once I was satisfied, I leaned down and swirled my tongue over the tip of his cock.

"Fuck," he gasped. "Please, please," he begged.

"Please what, witchling?" I asked, even though I knew exactly what he wanted.

He wanted me to mate with him. He wanted me to seal our bond, the one that we had just found.

I was fighting a war with myself every time he begged. I was quickly realizing just how hard it would be to resist truly falling for either one of them.

Is that what I wanted?

I took the head of Calen's cock between my lips, watching his entire body bow against Art. Art's arms tightened around him, his muscles rippling.

Beneath that suit and tie, he had a very nice body. One that I wanted to torture.

I'd been enjoying being single and only feeding when I absolutely had to. I'd enjoyed being in control of just myself, only worrying about how I felt. I'd made my goals and had met them. I was a good boss, independent and strong and caring.

I made my parents proud. I made my family proud.

But still...

This was different.

Art was watching me, studying me. I could feel the hum of his magic as I began to suck Calen. It was like a soft blanket, but one that had threads that sometimes shocked me.

Two witches and a monster.

Fuck.

I let out a little groan, forgetting everything. I didn't need to think about our worries right now. I just needed to focus on this moment.

Calen and Art were what mattered.

And hell, I mattered too.

"Please," Calen whined again. "Please. I want to feel you around me."

"Teeth and all?" I asked, fighting off a little smirk.

"Yes," he rasped. "I trust you."

He was so sweet. He wanted this, to be touched and loved and wanted.

"I can take the weight," Art said. "Fucking crush me for all I care, this is heaven. And my knot isn't going down."

I grinned now, pleased. I rose and moved my leg over Calen and Art, straddling them. I felt the tip of Calen's cock against my entrance, and I felt the snap of possession.

I wanted to mate him. I wanted to seal the bond and tie him to me forever, whatever the consequences may be.

Fuck it. What would the consequences be?

I began to lower myself, Calen's cock sliding inside. We groaned together.

He felt too fucking good. I'd been with plenty of partners, but this was different.

Heat stabbed through me and I gasped, sinking down lower.

Art surprised us by thrusting his hips up, thus thrusting Calen too. The two of us gasped as I took more of Calen's cock, followed by a deep chuckle from Art.

"You're stunning," Calen breathed, his eyes like little golden moons. He watched me with reverence, with devout appreciation.

I could see my reflection there, and I was his monstrous goddess. My wings spread behind me as I started to ride his cock, enjoying the hitches in his breath as the teeth scraped over his shaft.

He liked a little pain, I realized.

I began to move up and down, the sound of our skin meeting filling my room. I kept my eyes on him, my teeth sharpening.

I wanted to taste his blood. I was desperate for it.

Fuck.

"Mate me," Calen pleaded. "Please. Please, Inferna. I want you. I don't care what happens, but I want you."

"Fuck," Art growled. "Already, Calen?"

I hesitated, my pussy clenching around him. I was truly fighting myself now.

All it would take was one bite. The teeth around my entrance clamping onto him, locking us in place, and...

He would be mine.

"We just met," I whispered, a low growl leaving me.

"I don't care," he rasped. "Fuck, I don't care. *Please.* Please take me. I can feel that I'm yours."

Art growled some, his eyes meeting mine.

He belonged to Art too, that was undeniable now that the three of us had been together.

But did Art belong to me?

Art growled again, but then his eyes shut and I watched as pleasure overcame him again.

I looked back at Calen and sucked in a breath. A tear slipped free from his eyes and I moaned.

"Witchling," I said. "Are you certain?"

"Yes," he whispered.

I leaned forward, taking his cock completely as our lips met. He groaned, taking my kiss. I scraped my teeth over his bottom lip and then kissed down his jaw to the pulse in his neck.

He gasped as he felt my muscles tighten around his cock, the teeth scraping his skin.

"Oh fuck," he breathed.

Art groaned beneath us and I spared him a glance before gripping Calen's head, turning it to the side, and sinking my teeth into his neck just as the teeth around my pussy sank into his cock.

He screamed, but within seconds it turned into cries of pleasure. An orgasm crashed into both of us and I felt his cum filling me, my own muscles spasming.

The first taste of his blood hit like a heavy drug, our bodies humming as the connection was created. I felt his magic, his wants, his desires.

Fuck. I could taste *him*.

My mate.

I groaned and drank his blood, feeding on the high of lust. He tasted sweet, like fucking perfection.

Calen's cock began to swell inside of me, and I felt us lock together just like he and Art were. I pulled my fangs free of his neck and then looked down at Art, a drop of blood falling from my lips to his.

He groaned and licked it away, his eyes widening. "Fuck, you're beautiful. Everything feels so good."

"I know," I whispered.

Calen was gasping now and I felt his heat finally start to lessen, only a little.

I kissed him, cupping his face. "You did so good," I whispered.

"I'm yours," Calen whimpered.

"You are," I said, feeling that all the way to the roots of my soul.

This was crazy, but I didn't care.
Even if Art wasn't mine, Calen was.

CHAPTER EIGHT
horny resources

ART

I stepped into the elevator, heading towards my new office. I was early this morning, way earlier than I had intended.

I had snuck out of Inferna's apartment this morning, despite feeling my gut twist at leaving the two of them.

I had to clear my head.

I had stayed the night, sleeping next to them and breaking a rule that I had kept for years.

After the two of us had locked ourselves to Calen last night, the three of us had fallen asleep together. In the middle of the night, my knot had slipped free. Then Inferna and I had cleaned up Calen, bathed him, and then put him back to sleep.

Every muscle in my body was a bit sore, but...

I had enjoyed every moment of what had happened, even if it made me feel uncertain.

Another creature stepped into the elevator behind me, a

massive muscled griffin. He wore a crisp plaid shirt and slacks, and he held a bagel and cup of coffee in his claws.

"Nine, please," he grumbled.

I arched a brow and hit the button.

"What's your name?" I asked.

The griffin turned to look at me, looking me up and down. "Ah, hell, you're the Warts boss."

"I am," I said, my tone becoming cold.

"You took our coffee pot."

"Well, it looks like it won't matter now that we're all in the same office together, right?" I snipped.

"I guess," he grumbled. "My name is Poppins. I'm one of the bug specialists for Claws."

I nodded, offering him a bland smile. I didn't like talking to people right when I walked in, especially people that in theory worked for me.

The elevator took us to our floor, our new office. We both stepped out and I paused, taking in the sight.

Fucking hell. Inferna was not going to be happy.

Hell, I wasn't happy.

"Mr. Snakeroot, I presume," a curt voice said.

I turned to see a woman standing to the right of Poppins and me. She wore a black pencil skirt and a blazer, a soft pink blouse underneath. She was undoubtedly a vampire, based on the prim fanged smile she offered me.

It wasn't a happy smile. It was a cunning one.

This wasn't what I wanted to walk into this morning. I hadn't slept much last night and while today was a big day, I hadn't expected the fucking HR representative to be here at the ass crack of office hours.

"Yes, that is me," I said, pulling on the charm. I oozed charisma, calm and collected, and most definitely not thinking about knotting Calen again. "And you are?"

"I'm Alice, your HR rep. I'm here to help with the transition. Where is Inferna?"

"I am not sure," I lied. Why was I lying for her? "The office doesn't open until 9 a.m., and I am here early only because I wanted to check on things."

"Hmmm," Alice hummed, drawing out a pen from her blazer pocket and scribbling on a notepad.

I arched a dark brow. "Inferna will be here soon, I'm sure, can't say I know her very well."

"Interesting," Alice said, scribbling more.

Now, I glared a little harder.

"Well, since you are here early, we can discuss some things. Let me show you to your new office. And as for you," Alice said, looking at Poppins. "You are not salaried and should not be in the office this early. Please head down to the cafeteria."

"I was just going to wait at my desk," Poppins said sourly.

I gave him an almost pleading glance, but he wasn't focused on me.

Alice arched a blonde brow. "Not negotiable."

"What the fuck?" Poppins growled, but he turned and hit the elevator button.

"Hmm," Alice said, scribbling on her notepad again.

She was already pissing me off beyond reason.

"What are you taking notes on?" I asked.

"Notes about what will need to change. Already, I see several problems. Starting with you not correcting him for using foul language. That is unacceptable in the workplace."

I fought the urge to laugh at her because her face said she was dead serious.

"Alice," I said, trying to keep my tone pleasant. "With

all due respect, Poppins here isn't on the clock yet, as you so kindly pointed out. I am also in need of a bit of caffeine before we get into heavy details and would prefer to wait for Inferna, considering it might concern her."

"Hmm."

I should have grabbed Inferna's number so I could warn her that our HR rep was a bitchy vampire that already seemed determined to fire me.

Alice raised her head, giving me a very fake smile. "Coffee then?"

"Yes," I said, turning down the hall.

I went through to the office, pausing to take everything in. This floor was almost identical to my own, but now there was even less space. Tables were spread out with monitors, and I could see names on each seat.

"Assigned seating?" I asked, fighting the urge to argue.

"Yes. Each seating arrangement is nonnegotiable while we work on the transition."

"Great," I said, gritting my teeth. "Where's the espresso machine we were promised?"

Alice sighed, annoyed. "It's in the kitchenette. We installed a sparkling water machine too. So many benefits for employees."

I fought the urge to laugh at her and strode across the office to the kitchenette. The espresso machine awaited, already loaded up. I ignored the sound of a pen on paper as I pulled out a cup and started it up, making a fresh whipped latte.

Sure, it wouldn't be as great as a coffee shop but it was still better than what I could do.

More scribbling noises. I grit my teeth and then took a sip of my latte, turning to look at Alice. "So, how long do you expect to be here?"

"As long as necessary. There is a lot of paperwork that needs to be done, along with employee evaluations," Alice said, still making notes. "There was a report that was put in recently that we will need to discuss."

"A report?" I asked.

"Yes," Alice said curtly. "But we will wait for Inferna. I assume she gets here early?"

"Every day," I lied. "We sometimes end up on the elevator together."

Me and my silver tongue. It was a good thing I was a witch.

"Hmm."

Fucking hell. Could I say anything right?

I took another sip of coffee, mulling things over.

There were quite a few things that one learned when they became a manager. One, how to manage people. Two, was the list of things you don't do as a manager.

You don't curse at people, you don't tell them they're an idiot even if they are.

You don't sleep with the other office boss and then knot your employee.

I swallowed hard, clearing my throat.

"Don't worry, Arthur," Alice said, still scrawling like she was a fucking scribe. "If there's anything that needs to be fixed, we will get it there."

"Are you an HR rep or an exterminator?" I asked, laughing.

The laugh was forced and my words certainly came out a lot more seriously than I had intended.

Alice arched a brow, pausing her writing. "Hmm."

Oh, for fuck's sake.

"Right. I am going to go to the restroom. Is there anyone I need to thank for moving all of our stuff?"

"Nope," she said.

"Okay then," I huffed, leaving the kitchenette quickly.

I rounded the corner, damn near running straight into none other than Inferna.

I let out a little hiss, immediately grabbing her by her shoulders and shoving her back. She started to speak, but I covered her mouth— shoving her into the men's bathroom.

Her teeth sank into my hand and I fought a yelp, pulling back.

"WHAT THE—"

"SHHH." I hushed, covering her mouth again. "For god's sake woman," I hissed. "Shut up. HR is here."

"So you fucking shoved me into the restroom?" Inferna snarled. "What the fuck, Art?"

I glanced at the door nervously. "She's a vampire," I whispered.

"So?" Infera snapped.

"She keeps saying hmm a lot. She's bad news, I can tell you that."

"Art," Inferna hissed. "Listen, we just have to do this. Play like we like each other."

"Do we still hate each other?" I asked, suddenly painfully aware that our bodies were pressed together.

Fuck. I couldn't think about her in bed right now. I couldn't think about how fucking good Calen had looked between us.

"I'm taking a half-day today," Inferna said. "Calen too. He may be able to make it a few hours, but his heat hasn't broken. He's going to use a spell."

"Fucking hell," I whispered. "We're fucked. Alice is going to devour us."

"I'm sure it will be fine," Inferna snapped. "Come on."

I ground my teeth together but ultimately, left the bathroom first, glancing both ways. The office spread out in front of me, the silence eerie.

"Arthur?" Alice called.

Inferna slipped out of the bathroom behind me, moving around me with a little growl. "Fucking imbecile."

"Hey," I growled, but I followed after her.

Inferna rounded the corner, heading for the kitchenette. Alice was still waiting and lifted her head, giving another fake smile to Inferna.

"Inferna," she said. "Nice to meet you."

"Nice to meet you, Alice," Inferna purred.

Why the fuck was her reaction so much nicer!?

"Arthur said that you're always early, and I'm happy to hear that. We have some things we must go over," Alice said. "Starting with your new roles."

"New roles?" Inferna and I asked.

I took a breath and fought off a groan. I caught a whiff of Inferna's perfume and I dug my nails into my palm, urging my cock not to harden.

I hated her, I reminded myself. She was annoying and smart and sexy and fuck...

That didn't sound like hate.

"I have all the paperwork. Let's head to your new office space."

Inferna and I stole an uneasy glance at each other and then followed Alice across the space, heading straight for another room. We stepped inside, immediately met with the same bland decoration they always gave us. At least my office had always had character.

I took one glance at the poster that said 'You're only a leader once you've made a leader who has made a leader' and fought the urge to groan. It was plastered over the picture of a golf course, which made zero fucking sense.

"Well, I see that it was decorated for us," Inferna said flatly.

"Yes. With company approved decoration," Alice said curtly. "We would like to keep things consistent. Have a seat."

There was one desk with two chairs on one side, and one on the other.

Alice took the one chair, forcing Inferna and me into the other two.

Inferna crossed one leg over the other, adjusting in her seat. "What is going on, Alice? Today, we are merging but this feels like a lot more."

Alice adjusted herself in her seat, laying down her notepad and pen. She then reached down, drawing up a briefcase. The silence settled around us, stuffy and uncomfortable.

Inferna's tail flicked back and forth out of the corner of my eye, her fake smile almost worse than Alice's.

Alice drew out several sheets of paper and then raised her head, looking at us both with her crimson eyes. "Warts & Claws is growing, but with growth, there comes change. We do not need two leaders in this office. We only need one. Essentially, we will be interviewing all employees about what they think of you. We will be cross-examining, looking for any red flags. If anything is out of line, you will be promptly removed from your position."

I was speechless.

I had worked my ass off to get where I was. I wasn't a witch of stature, I hadn't come from a rich family. I had worked my way to the top, risen from the ashes of the dark past that plagued my coven.

Inferna made a noise, and part of me wished she would

throw a fit. Part of me wished she was temperamental enough to walk straight out.

But, she didn't

"I know that this might come as a shock. I know that it might feel unfair. And that is what I am here for," Alice said, giving us a pleasant smile. "I am here to help with the transition."

"What do you need from us, then, Alice?" Inferna asked, her voice cold.

"I need both of you to read through these contracts and to carefully look over the agreements in the behavior zone. Foul language, discussing personal lives, and having a relationship with your coworkers is forbidden."

Fuck. I thought about Calen, fighting to keep my expression calm and pleasant.

Alice knew she was making us nervous. She was a vampire. She could hear my heartbeat just like I could read through her fucking false words.

"You mentioned that there was a report made," I said.

Inferna looked up at me and then back at Alice. "Report?"

Alice nodded. "There was an anonymous complaint in regards to there being sexual misconduct in the work environment. It did not say whom, merely that there were... things happening."

Inferna scoffed. "There have never been such activities in my office."

"That you know of," Alice said coldly, turning her eyes on me.

Fuck. Did someone really report Calen and me?

We'd used the right spells. And there was always technically a reason to have him in my office.

Still, witches weren't idiots. I'm sure that some of the

more energy-attuned witches could read our auras. Hell, hadn't Sally whipped out tarot cards and warned me about Inferna?

Was Inferna bad for me?

And if she was, why had last night been so fucking good?

"Well," I said, clearing my throat. "I'm sure that... we will have a smooth transition."

"Of course," Alice chirped. "That's why I'm here."

CHAPTER NINE
tuesday tails

CALEN

I sat down at my new desk and fought the urge to run straight for Inferna and Art and demand that they fuck me again.

My entire body, even with a heavy glamor and completely spelled, was reacting to their scents in the room alone. I watched as the vampy HR rep led Inferna and Art through the office, the three of them chatting like they didn't hate each other's guts.

I needed HR to leave. I needed them to leave so I could get fucked over Art's new desk.

The pixie demon girl sitting across from me shook her head, turning her focus back on her screen. "This is a crock of bullshit."

"It is," I mumbled. "I have nothing against monsters though. Not like some of the witches."

She sighed, shrugging. "I don't really care about witches. I don't have some of the problems others have had.

I know there are bad covens out there but there are also terrible monsters. What's your name?"

"Calen," I said, swallowing hard.

She crinkled her nose, her full black eyes studying me. Our tables were pressed against each other, our monitors back to back. "Calen. My name is Loralie, but you can call me Lora."

I gave her a smile, feeling sweat roll down my back.

Fucking hell.

There was another monster and witch in our corner. One of the witches that I didn't talk to often, Hazard, and then a manticore who had yet to spare me a second glance. He was too busy listening to music at full blast from his headphones.

Hazard arched a brow, giving me a knowing look. He was one of the best spell casters in the city, but he was the quiet and broody type.

"Calen," Lora said. "Are you okay? You look really pale. No offense, but if you're sick, you should go home. Today's a big day for the company but that's what sick days are for."

"We don't have sick days," Hazard said. "Not really. We have to use personal time."

"What the fuck?" Lora scoffed. "They better not make that a policy. We have sick time. Everyone should have sick time. Can't you use your spells to change that?"

Hazard barked out a laugh. "No, princess, that's not how that fucking works."

Lora's demeanor changed almost instantly, her expression becoming hostile and pinning directly on Hazard.

The heat was starting to rise up again. I tried to focus on the chatter around us, but all I could think about was my mate.

Fuck. I had a mate.

My cock twitched in my pants and this time, Lora and the manticore turned to look at me.

The manticore slid his headphones off, drawing in a little huff of air. "Listen," he said, "I just come here to work. But I can't sit next to you if you're going to smell like *that*."

"Like..like what?" I asked, swallowing hard.

Lora shook her head, standing. "Fuck this. I refuse to be stuck with three men, especially one in fucking heat. I didn't even know witches do that, but it's irresponsible to just waltz around—"

I stood up, my chair screeching back. The whole office fell silent, eyes turning on me.

FUCK.

I caught Inferna's sharp gaze from across the room and she excused herself from Art and the HR vamp, heading straight for me.

Everyone's attention immediately swiveled on her and for the first time, I could truly appreciate that she was a succubus.

"Hello, creatures," Inferna said, giving everyone a wicked smile.

I felt the push from her, our bond tightening.

Go hide in my office.

I drowned out her words, escaping everyone's attention quickly while she had it. I went across the floor, skating past Art and Alice without them paying attention to me as well.

The moment I made it to the separate boss office, I shut the door behind me and let out a breath. My glamor immediately fell and my knees buckled, the heat rising through my body.

"Fuck this," I breathed.

Being an omega was torture. My cock started to harden, the mating bite around the base aching.

It wasn't the fucking bite at my neck that had sealed my fate, it was the one from my Mistress' pussy.

The office door shut and I turned with a gasp, and then let out a breath. Art shook his head, coming straight to me.

"Today is a fucking nightmare," he hissed.

"I'm so fucking hard," I whined. "I can't stop. I can't."

Arthur flicked his hand, sending up a very powerful spell. One that no creature, at least not one in this city, should be able to step through.

And yet, the door flew open and we both gaped as Inferna stepped in.

The door shut behind her and she shook her head. "Fucking hell, today is awful. I sent everyone off to lunch, including that fucking HR bitch. She's out for our balls."

Art growled. "One of us is going to lose our job."

Inferna stepped forward and I was pulled to standing and then pushed towards the desk, then on top. I gasped, surprised by the two of them.

Art growled again but was already undoing his pants.

"It'll be you," Inferna snapped at him. "Fucking moron. One of your Warts witches reported the two of you and now we have to watch our backs."

I gasped as office supplies were swiped off the desktop, pens and sticky notes flying. Inferna was already undoing my belt and Art's cock was already out and hard.

"Fuck his throat, Art," Inferna snapped. "And make it quick. I can't go home early today because of that vampire, so we're going to fuck him hard enough that he can survive till the end of the day."

I moaned, gasping as my pants were yanked down and my cock sprang free.

Art climbed onto the desk, straddling my chest. I

opened my mouth to speak, but instead— Art shoved the head of his cock inside.

I groaned, a muffled scream leaving me as I felt the cold gel of lube dripped onto my skin. Inferna's tail rubbed it and then moved down to my ass.

For a split second, I wondered where she got lube, and she answered with a chuckle. "Kept some in my pocket today just in case."

She shoved my legs back and I screamed as the two of them plunged into me at the same time, her hand wrapping around my cock. I choked, dragging in air through my nose as Art started to thrust in and out of my mouth.

"Good boy," Inferna purred. "Such a good boy taking us like this. You've been so needy. I could smell you through your spells, just begging to be fucked by your mate."

Art grunted, his hands planted on the desk above my head. "Fuck, you feel good. You're both driving me crazy."

Inferna's seductive chuckle had me moaning as she stroked my cock. Her tail fucked me in the same rhythm that Art took my throat and I felt myself get closer and closer to the edge.

Fuck, I needed to cum. I wished it could be inside Inferna again, that I could be locked inside her sweet heat. I groaned as she pumped me, the tip of her nail pressing against the head of my cock.

The little nip of pain was enough to send me spiraling.

Art gasped at the same time I gave a muffled yelp, his cum spilling into my mouth while my cum shot out onto Inferna. I swallowed, tears leaking out of the corners of my eyes as Art pulled his cock free, sitting back on my chest.

Inferna's tail pulled free and I melted against the desk, panting.

"Feel better?" Inferna asked, coming around to look down at me.

I nodded, panting. "For now. I can breathe now."

It was true. I at least didn't feel like I was on fire.

"Good," Inferna said, grinning down at me. "Let's get cleaned up and work on a stronger spell."

CHAPTER TEN
magical meetings

INFERNA

I'd had my mate for lunch and felt fully satisfied as I joined the next miserable meeting.

Alice had so politely informed us that we would each be attending classes while our employees were interviewed. I seriously wanted to question the thought process behind these bastard decisions, and also why it was okay for her to be talking to people alone.

There was something very wrong with the entire situation. It was hard to think clearly, though, when my freshly bitten mate was in heat and I was slowly becoming more and more determined to seduce Art.

I liked the way he looked, submissive and breedable. Watching him fuck Calen had made my blood burn.

I glanced up at him from across our office.

We had decided to shove another desk in here, both still living with the title of boss like it was going to drag us across the finish line.

I needed to call my papa after work and ask for advice before I gutted this company from the inside out. Starting with Alice, the vampire that had shown up from the HR department from hell.

I thought about some of the vampire friends I had, wondering if I'd be able to find some tea on her.

Maybe. I needed to give Minni a call anyway.

Art gave a long sigh and I looked up, finding that his eyes were on me.

The door to the office had been unscrewed and tossed by Alice after lunch. The little vampire had hauled that thing through the office like it was a paperclip, took it down the elevator, and then I'd watched her throw it in the garbage from the windows.

Open door policy, she'd said like it was the neatest thing since sliced bread.

Fuck my life.

Art arched a brow, tearing his gaze away. I did the same, refocusing on the creature that was talking on the screen. I'd muted him two minutes in once I'd realized it was pre-recorded and that it was just a general overview of changes within the company.

The headliner was that we were all fucked.

The job I'd worked my ass off for had successfully launched itself into a shit pit.

It *was* an HR issue that they were going to fire Art or me, but I couldn't get ahold of anyone that wasn't Alice. Someone was too busy sucking dick and ignoring phone calls.

I could feel Calen getting restless again, our bond tightening some. After Art and I had fucked him senseless, Art worked with him to create an even stronger suppressant spell. One that would have even blinded me if I hadn't been his mate.

Part of me wondered why I was here. Big day or not, I had someone else to care for...

I wanted to be back in bed with Calen in my arms. Getting up and ready for work this morning had been one of the hardest things I'd ever had to do.

We had two hours left in the day and then we could go home.

A soft knock had me looking up to see Anne. She gave me a pained smile and I gave her a nod, watching as she scurried over towards me.

"What's up?" I whispered, frowning.

Anne came around to my seat, her back to Art and her expression falling as she talked in a hushed whisper. "There are some problems."

I frowned. "Well, we knew..."

"No," Anne whispered, shaking her head. "Legitimate problems. Loralie was just interviewed by Alice and once she got out, she hasn't spoken since. Something is wrong."

I scowled, feeling a prickle of worry.

Loralie was one of the strongest women that I knew. She wasn't the type to go silent either.

"It happened to one of the witches too," Anne whispered.

"*Who?*" I asked, my voice tightening.

If Alice upset Calen, then she was a dead woman. HR rep or not.

It was still a monstrous world and if she fucked with my mate—

A low growl left me.

Anne put her hand on my shoulder, giving me a tight smile. "HR is about to walk in," she breathed, immediately standing up and moving away just as Alice waltzed through the door.

Alice looked over at us, her eyes narrowing.

"Yes, ma'am," Anne said, giving me the brightest smile she could muster. "I know that meeting is a lot, I'll make sure you have a fresh cup of coffee and some new pens to make notes with. Let me know if you need anything else."

"Thank you, Anne," I said sweetly, flashing my fangs.

Anne grinned and if I hadn't worked with her for so long, I wouldn't have known any different.

Alice's gaze flickered as my receptionist passed by, skirting out into the main part of the office.

"Well, how are interviews going?" I asked Alice.

She ignored me, looking at Art. "Do you have Calen's file?"

Art raised his head and I felt my blood turn cold.

"All of the files are where they should be," Art answered, arching a brow.

He was a lot better at playing calm and collected.

"His file is missing," Alice said.

"Interesting. I can't say I know where else it might be," Art said, leaning back in his chair.

There was a devilish charm about him when he took on this persona, the one that I liked a little more than I cared to admit.

"Is that not HR's job to keep a digital file? We've been past paper record keeping only for awhile, Alice," Art said.

Alice cocked her head and I could feel the tension. I cleared my throat. "I have to say the same for Claws. We've been past primarily paper keeping for awhile. I'm sure that Mr. Snakeroot's secretary could help."

Alice looked at me, back at Art, and then straightened her shoulders. "Well. We shall see."

With that, she left the room again.

Art's jaw stiffened and he shook his head, looking up at me. "I'm about to lose it."

"Me too," I breathed. "Not to mention, I'm pretty certain they lost all of my personal art supplies when they moved us. I want to be back at my old office. Also, this is throwing off our productivity. Not just mine, but the entire office."

"And you know she'll hold us accountable for that," Art snorted, rubbing his face. "We're fucked."

"Oh, but be sure not to say fuck," I said sarcastically.

"Ah yes," Art said, his lips twisting into a smirk. "I shouldn't say fuck, should I? What was that all about with Anne?"

I arched my brow, snorting. He had slipped that question in smoother than I had anticipated. "Trouble," I said, standing up.

Less than two hours left in the day, I reminded myself. "Arthur," I said, moving towards his desk. I glanced at the doorway, making sure that Alice wasn't lingering. "Dinner tonight," I said, looking at him. "My apartment."

"Is that a command?" he asked.

"Yes," I said. "We need to have a meeting. I'm going to go check on one of my people."

Arthur nodded, his eyes flashing with concern. "I can't get ahold of anyone. I feel like we're being held hostage."

I nodded, the wheels in my head turning.

There was definitely something wrong, but there wasn't much we could do.

Not yet, anyway.

I stretched my neck for a moment and then left our office, stepping out onto the floor. A couple of my creatures raised their heads, giving me a look that I didn't like.

Even a couple of the witches glanced at me and then away.

I drew up the persona, the seductive easy going one that I wore like a second skin. I strode across the office, heading straight for Poppin's table.

He turned in his seat, arching a feathered brow. "Hey Boss. Today has been shit," he whispered.

"I know," I said, looking around for Alice.

One of the witches sitting across from Poppins leaned in, his eyes a dark forest green. "One of your Claws is in the bathroom crying," he whispered. "Everyone is stressed. Can you and Arthur not argue with corporate?"

I winced. "It's complicated. We've been given ultimatums too," I said.

"I'm just going to quit if it gets more stressful," the witch sighed, shaking his head. "Fucking stupid."

"I agree. Poppins," I said, softening my voice. "Keep an ear to the ground."

He nodded, his shoulders squaring up. "Will do, Boss."

I skirted around their table, heading towards the bathrooms. I pushed open the door, stepping inside.

Loralie was sitting on the counter, her expression blank. To my surprise, a witch was standing next to her, consoling her.

"Lora," I said, frowning. "Are you okay?"

She looked up at me, shaking her head.

"Fuck," I sighed.

"Let me put up an anti-listening spell," the witch whispered.

"Thank you," I said, glancing at the door. "What's your name? I'm Inferna."

"I'm Gemmi," she said, giving me a little smile.

"Loralie, what happened?" I asked. "Anne told me that something happened."

"There's something wrong with that vampire," she answered, looking up at me. Her piercing glinted in the bathroom lighting and at some point, she had swept her silvery hair back into a bun. Her onyx eyes were wide, her cheeks flushed. "I don't know. She questioned me about you and Art. And then she asked about omega witches and I only know of one, that guy in my group."

It took every ounce of control not to lose my temper. "She asked about omega witches?"

"Yeah. And I told her she was stupid because I didn't even know that was a thing for witches," Loralie said, shaking her head.

"It's kind of rare," Gemmi chimed in. "But it can happen. Monsters and witches are basically the same."

"That's what I keep saying," Loralie mumbled. "Anyway, I don't know. It was weird, Inferna. She's got something out for you or for the witch boss. I'm not sure what."

"Fucking hell," I sighed, shaking my head. "This has been the longest day in the office."

"It has been," they both agreed.

"Well," I said. "Keep your head down. Try not to attract attention. And if you need anything, you can trust Art too if I'm not around. He's not as terrible as I thought."

They both nodded and I pressed my lips together, patting Loralie's shoulder.

"You promise you will come find me if you need me, right?" I asked.

"Yes," she said. She then scowled, baring her little pixie fangs. Her stained glass wings fluttered a little behind her back, her veins turning black beneath her skin. "If she wants to fight, we can fight."

Gemmi gave Loralie a little pat. "Now, now, pixie girl. We don't need any mischief or fights right now."

Lora grumbled, shaking her head.

With that, I left the two of them, heading back out onto the floor.

The mood was weird, and I didn't like it.

Not to mention...

I hadn't seen Calen.

My heart gave a little pound and I looked around.

"Hey."

I looked up. Art moved towards me, his bright blue eyes angry. He stopped when he got to me, looking around.

"Where is Calen?" I asked. "Do you know?"

"I bet Alice has him since she was looking for his file. Let's go barge in," Art growled.

Fuck it. We were going to crash their little interview, and at this point— I didn't even care if I walked out of here without a job today.

I was the boss, but I was done being the boss if that meant I had to let someone treat my team like shit.

CHAPTER ELEVEN
no flying fucks

ART

I felt the last of my fucks given fly away as Inferna and I opened the door to the small, secluded office that the HR vamp had sequestered our mate in.

And fuck it. Fuck everything. Even if Calen wasn't mine completely yet, he was still *mine*.

And one extra *fuck it*. I'd hated Inferna's guts but now we had a new enemy, and she was smiling like an evil bitch next to me.

"What the fuck is the meaning of this?" Inferna hissed.

Alice growled, baring her fangs at us.

Calen was strapped down to a chair, unmoving. There was an aura around him, one that made me feel sick just being in its presence. It radiated from a crystal on the desktop, a disgusting shade of green emanating from it.

"The two of you aren't supposed to be in here," Alice hissed.

Inferna lunged across the room, her tail knocking the crystal off the desktop and her hands wrapping around Alice's throat. The two of them moved in a blur, but even though Alice was a vampire— she wasn't a match for Inferna.

Calen slumped to the side and I caught him before he hit the floor, my heart pounding in my chest.

"What the fuck did you do to him?!" Inferna yelled. "What kind of fucked up HR person are you?! I will absolutely end your fucking career and your god damned life!" Inferna sneered.

Alice hissed, baring her fangs again. "Let me go!"

"Inferna," I said, struggling to keep my tone even. "Inferna, Calen is okay. He's okay," I said again, looking down at him.

He wasn't great, but he was okay.

And hard again.

Fucking hell. Being an omega was a curse.

I glanced up at the doorway, hearing the movement of others in the office heading towards us.

"Take him home," Inferna said coldly, never pulling her gaze from Alice.

There was something entirely too erotic about watching a boss like Inferna pin an outrageous HR rep to the wall like a bug.

"Take him home, Art. Now. I'll handle everything else. Have dinner ready by 6:30 p.m. sharp, too."

"Yes, ma'am," I breathed.

I didn't hesitate, drawing a circle around Calen and me. I felt the magic hit my veins, the burning thrill rushing through me as I took both of us through a portal.

We landed in Inferna's living room and Calen groaned beneath me.

I took a breath and then looked down at him, realizing I was on top and that our cocks were pressed together.

I breathed in his scent, closing my eyes.

I wasn't supposed to be thinking about fucking him again. I wasn't supposed to be thinking about how good it had felt to knot him.

"I'm okay," Calen rasped. "That stone had bad magic. But I'm okay. And fuck, I need you right now."

"Calen," I rasped, cupping his face. "What happened?"

His eyes widened and he let out a little breath. His skin was hot again, his cheeks flushed. He still looked like he was running a fever despite Inferna and me fucking him on the desk earlier.

He reached up, raking his fingers through my neatly combed beard. He gave it a little rub, mussing it.

"She was trying to break into my mind using the stone," he whispered.

"I didn't think vampires could do magic," I growled, shaking my head.

"They can if they know the right witches. I don't know. I can't remember what she said to me," Calen whined. He thrust his hips up, rubbing our cocks together through our slacks. "*Please.*"

I gave another low growl, but my blood still rushed from my head straight down *there*.

"Calen," I groaned. "You fucking omega. I'm trying to make sure you're okay."

"And I want you to boss me around," he breathed, giving another little thrust. "I want you to use your belt on me. Make me ready for our Mistress for when she gets home. Make me cum all over myself."

My breath hitched and I leaned back, straddling him.

Calen was too cute for me to say no to.

I'd already left work to bring him here. Me, the boss of the fucking Warts office, a witch that lived and breathed work culture, had left work for *him*.

For Inferna too.

For a moment, I worried. Would she be okay handling Alice?

She's seemed pretty damn capable.

Calen reached down between us and with the flick of a skilled finger, his magic pulled down my fly. I huffed out a laugh and shook my head, standing up.

We were on Inferna's living room floor, the rug beneath our feet soft and plush. I knew it was good for kneeling because my knees had been there last night when she had made me crawl.

This week had gone to hell and heaven.

"On your knees," I growled.

Calen's golden eyes widened and he rolled over, making a little pout with his lips.

I held his gaze and slid my hands down to my belt, slowly unclasping it. The metal clinked, sounding like a little bell as I undid it.

The room was silent now, aside from the sound of the leather sliding across my belt loops.

Calen shivered, his breath catching. "Please," he whimpered.

"You were just being practically tortured by a crazy HR vampire," I said, tossing my belt to the floor. "And now all you can think about is my cock. About me breeding you like a little slut."

"Yes," he gasped, his expression pleading. "Yes. I need you. Fuck, I'm already so hard."

"You just want my knot," I chuckled, enjoying the way he bit his bottom lip as I let my pants go to the floor, and my cock free.

He sucked in a breath, a little moan leaving him.

I couldn't be mad or frustrated when this little witchling was all mine.

I thought about Inferna too.

I would need to make sure he was all ready for her. I wanted to please her, to make her proud.

Would she be proud if I left marks on his ass? Or would she be mad?

My cock pulsed and I ran my palm over my shaft, groaning at the feel of the ridges. Calen licked his lips, giving me those fucking puppy eyes.

"Open your mouth," I growled.

He obeyed, tilting his head up and parting his sweet lips. I could see the outline of his cock in his pants, his skin gleaming beneath his button down.

I loosened my tie around my neck, pulling it free and then stepping towards him.

"Hands above your head and wrists together," I demanded.

I commanded and he obeyed. He lifted them over his head, his eyes now completely feasting on my throbbing cock. I ran the silk tie over his skin, enjoying every little noise he made.

My life had gone absolutely sideways this week, but I couldn't find myself giving a damn.

This was worth it. Seeing Calen on his knees, binding him with my neck tie. I let out a little groan as I put it over his wrists and tightened the loop, letting his hands fall down into his lap.

"Such a good boy," I whispered, cupping his face. I slid my thumb into his open mouth, smirking.

"Yes, Boss," he moaned, swirling his tongue over my skin.

My breath hitched, my cock hardening even more.

I loved it when he called me boss.

"Call me that again," I said.

"Boss," Calen rasped, giving my thumb a little bite.

"Do you want to be bred by your boss?" I asked, pulling my hand free and giving his face a gentle slap.

"Yes," he groaned. "Please. Please breed me, Boss."

"You want your boss to breed and knot your omega ass?" I growled.

His eyes fluttered, a long moan leaving him. "Please," he whispered. "I'm so fucking hard. How long am I going to stay like this?"

"Until Inferna and I can make it stop," I growled. "Your first heat and you're ours. You're mine. I'm going to breed and knot your ass and then I'm going to bathe you. Then we're going to cook dinner for our Mistress so she doesn't burn the building down. But first, let go of your glamor, little witchling. I want to see you in your truest form."

Calen's eyes softened and I watched him change, his pretty golden boy appearance melting into a much more monstrous one.

I loved him both ways.

My breath caught again. Did I just think about love?

"Please," Calen whispered. "Let me suck your cock. I want to taste you."

I ran my fingers to the back of his head, gripping his hair. I thrust my hips forward, my cock slipping between his lips. He grunted, his hands still lying in his lap as he let me use him.

My head tipped back, pleasure working through me. He

felt so fucking good, everything about his hot mouth was perfect.

I'd been with him many times but each one still felt new. And with this connection growing and growing...

A snarl left me and I lost the edge of my control for a moment, giving a hard pump and hitting the back of his throat. He choked a little, a groan leaving him as I eased back and then pumped into him again.

I fucked his throat, falling into a harsh rhythm. He took it so well, his eyes closing as I used him.

I felt myself so close to cumming and eased back, my blood burning with need.

"Get on all fours," I rasped, leaning over to pick up my belt.

Calen nodded, turning over onto all fours. His wrists were still bound by my tie and so he centered himself, balancing with his ass facing me.

He had a perfect ass. One that I wanted to spank and fuck over and over again.

The belt buckle jingled as I folded the leather, testing the snap of it on my palm. The sound of it on my skin echoed, and the sound alone also made my little omega groan.

"You're such a good boy," I whispered, stepping up behind him.

I leaned down, giving one of his ass cheeks a gentle squeeze. I needed to warm him up before spanking him. I started to rub his ass, giving small pats and slaps to each one until his skin started to warm beneath my hand.

"Boss," he whispered.

His cock was so hard and I admired the precum that dripped from the tip. I licked my lips, a hunger overtaking me.

When witches mated each other, there was a spell that was spoken. A sacred one. And not only was it sacred, it was unique to each pair. Even if we both had a relationship with the same person, such as Inferna, our bond would be unique. Just as my bond to her would be unique if we ever made one...

I felt the words on the tip of my tongue, the need to speak it becoming more and more pressing.

"Do you want me to mate you?" I whispered, giving his ass another slap.

Calen raised his head, looking at me over his shoulder. His golden eyes gleamed with need, his lips parting. "I do. I never thought you would want to."

"Me neither," I whispered.

It was true. I had lived the bachelor life for a long time. The life of a witch who was more dedicated to his job than actual pleasures. Sure, I'd been with others sexually but...

At the end of the day, I'd always cooked my own meals and ate them alone.

I'd wake up, work out, work at the office, cook dinner, and sleep.

Over and over again.

Then there was Calen.

He had interrupted my cycle.

And then there was Inferna.

And goddess knew, she had most certainly interrupted my pattern too.

"We'd be together forever," I said, swallowing hard.

"It's been a crazy week," Calen said, hanging his head. "But this is the first time in my life that I have been this happy. And fuck, I've known you longer than Inferna and she and I still mated each other."

"Right, but she's a little crazy," I chuckled.

"And we aren't?"

It was a fair point.

Plus, what was a timeline? For once in my life, I was going with the flow of things instead of intently plotting it out. For once, it wasn't about pros and cons— it was about what felt right.

Being with Calen felt right.

"I've wanted you since you hired me," Calen whispered.

I arched a brow, surprised to hear him say that.

"Since I hired you?" I asked, grinning. I gave his ass another slap and then gripped my belt.

"Yes," he said. "Since you sat across from me at your desk and interviewed me. I remember you asking me what my favorite type of magic was."

"And you said that you liked the wizard kind," I chuckled, giving him a little zap of my magic.

He groaned, his muscles tensing for a moment.

"Smart ass," I chuckled, "I'm going to spank you," I said.

"Please," he mumbled. "Please do."

"All those days of you watching me," I said, drawing my belt back. "I always noticed. And then finally, one day you ended up in my office. I was hard and needy," I said, patting his ass with my belt, teasing him. "Hard and needy and you were exactly what I needed. And now, you're all I fucking want."

"Please," Calen whimpered.

I smiled and this time when I drew my belt back, I struck his ass hard. He sucked in a breath, letting out a groan.

"Oh goddess," he gasped.

I struck him again, enjoying watching him take the hit

like a good omega witchling. I felt pleasure spread through me, the rush that I got from being the one in control.

Inferna had proved that I was definitely a switch. Being submissive to her while dominating Calen was perfect, feeding both parts of me. The hungry dominant part and the needy submissive one.

I struck him again, his cry ringing out. I let out a satisfied growl, hitting him again and then falling into a consecutive rhythm.

One, two, three, four, five, six, seven, eight, nine, ten.

I gave him a break, pulling back for a moment.

Calen panted, his ass now hot to the touch.

I couldn't hold back anymore. My cock was so hard and I tossed the belt to the side, moving up behind him.

"Are you going to be a good little boss's slut?" I asked.

"Yes," he rasped. "Yes, I'm all yours."

CHAPTER TWELVE

mates

CALEN

Art slowly eased his cock inside of me, both of us groaning together. I was so needy for him, my body humming with magic and heat.

My skin burned where he had spanked me, the sting of the leather still lingering. It had felt so good, the best type of pain.

I liked knowing that he had branded me. That I would see those marks later tonight.

His cock spread me, throbbing inside of me. Every inch made me gasp, his fingers raking down my back and then gripping my hips.

I looked back over my shoulder, at how lost he was in fucking me. His head was tipped back, his lips parted in ecstasy. His sleeves were rolled up, the front of his shirt open and revealing his hard chest and abs.

I groaned, my cock pulsing with every movement. Art slid in and out of me, setting a brutal pace.

I wanted his knot. I wanted to feel him inside of me, for this fire to finally be sated.

The sounds of our skin slapping together filled the room and I dug my fingers into the carpet, moaning. I loved the feeling of being taken by Art, of him dominating me so completely.

Especially after watching him submit to Inferna.

"I'm going to mate you," Art growled. "I'm going to tie you to me forever. I'm going to wake you up every morning before work and breed you, over and over again."

Fuck, I was so close to cumming. His words made me gasp, his voice driving me crazy.

"I'm not stopping until you cum. And then once you cum like a good little omega slut, I will fill you with my cum and knot you."

"Yes, boss," I cried out.

He thrust into me hard and it was enough to send me over the edge, my orgasm hitting hard. I shot hot ropes of cum, my back arching as I came.

Art groaned, his hips still moving in a brutal rhythm. I felt his knot spread me as he pumped into me one last time, swelling and tying us together. I gasped, collapsing beneath him as he started to cum with a loud groan.

He held me still, his fingers digging into my hips. His knot was hot and pulsing, the ridges of his shaft rubbing me. He kept cumming, his breaths becoming small desperate gasps.

I moaned, the edge of the fire within me finally cooling off enough for me to think straight.

"Good boy," Art purred, leaning over me.

His arms came around, holding me tight. He lay back, pulling me with him until the two of us were spread out on the floor on our sides, him spooning me.

My lungs were still heaving with pants, my skin hot to the touch. My body thrummed with pleasure, his knot hot.

"Mine," Art whispered, kissing my cheek and nuzzling me.

I made a little noise, preening under his attention. "I love it when you're like this," I whispered.

Art chuckled, nipping my ear. "My little omega. Who would have known? You're mine."

"I'm yours," I said back, shivering against him.

He kissed my cheek again and this time, I felt our magic start to bleed into each other. I could feel the spell, the one that would bind us together forever, on the tip of my tongue.

"Are you certain I'm what you want?" Art whispered.

"Yes," I said, swallowing hard. "You and Inferna. I'm yours. It's right and it's fate."

Art nodded, making a low hum. The words that came out of his mouth now were ancient, a language that neither one of us knew but that we both knew. I felt the rush of magic, the embers in my soul stirred.

He spoke the spell and I answered him, closing my eyes as the air snapped around us. His arms tightened around me, holding me close as the spell took root.

"Art," I breathed, the breath knocked out of me.

"My mate," he gasped.

I squeezed my eyes shut harder, goosebumps erupting across my skin. I could feel him, his heart and soul. I could feel the connection, fragile and new like a butterfly fresh out of a chrysalis.

I was his.

I was his mate.

A tear slipped down my cheek and Art moaned, kissing it away. "I love you," he whispered. "I promise I'll take care of you. That even though I can be an ass sometimes, you're all I will think about."

"I love you too," I wheezed.

My heartbeat leveled out now, my muscles relaxing. I sank against him, completely enthralled by the fact that I now had two mates.

I still wasn't sure why I'd gone into heat, or how I hadn't known I was an omega witch. But I didn't care. This was perfect.

Everything felt perfect.

I felt my connection with Inferna too, her soul reaching out to mine.

I loved her. I would worship the ground she walked on, kiss every single part of her over and over again.

Already, Art and Inferna were better together too...

Maybe...just maybe, things would work out.

Art moaned. "Fucking hell, you feel good, Calen."

"Thank you," I chuckled.

"How are you feeling?" Art asked, trailing his fingertips up my side.

"Good," I whispered. "Happy. More happy than I've ever been."

Art nodded, rubbing me gently. "I guess... I guess we did things backwards in a way but I don't have any family for you or Inferna to meet."

I twisted a little to look up at him, surprised. I'd never heard Art talk about family or really anyone in his life, and now that made more sense. My chest ached a little.

"I don't have many," I said, "But I think you'll like my mom. She's an old witch with a cozy coven in a small town. She's really good with animals and healing. I grew up surrounded by squirrels and deer and raccoons."

Art snorted. "That sounds delightful to me, actually."

"I wonder what Inferna's family is like. She mentioned her dads," I said, frowning a little.

Both of us were quiet for a moment. Fuck, we would need to meet her family.

And not one Dad to impress, but two.

"Well," Art chuckled. "I'm sure they will love you. Me — I'm not so sure about. The coven that I left was very bad and did terrible things to monsters. Fought them, killed them, hurt them. And while I'm no longer with them…"

"You obviously aren't like that," I said, fighting off a groan as Art moved against me, his knot tugging some. "You left them, which is very difficult to do."

"It is," Art whispered.

Silence fell between us again, and I found myself closing my eyes.

"You can sleep," Art murmured. "I'll get you up once my knot is finished. Then we'll make some dinner."

"Okay," I whispered, giving a sleepy nod.

Within a couple of minutes, I found myself slipping into a nicely knotted nap.

CHAPTER THIRTEEN
dinner

INFERNA

I made it home without murdering anyone, but before I went upstairs to my apartment to see Art and Calen— I called my dad.

"Inferna," he answered, his voice always a growl.

I got my gruffness from him, along with my horns and tail and succubus-ness.

"Hey, Daddy," I sighed.

"Who upset you, baby?" he snarled, immediately sensing that I was upset.

That was a hard question. Today had actually gone straight to hell, and now I was pretty certain I was going to end up fired.

"My company merged with another one, and they gave us an HR rep from hell. Like literally. I caught her using a crystal on my mate and—"

Oh fuck.

I wasn't supposed to tell him about that yet.

"YOUR WHAT?"

"Daddy," I groaned, "Daddy, listen. I wasn't going to tell you about that yet—"

"WHO THE FUCK IS HE? I'M —"

This time I growled, silencing him rather quickly. "Listen to me! I will introduce you to him when I am ready."

I heard my Papa in the background, his voice soothing my monstrous Dad.

He also successfully plucked the phone away, his sweet voice coming on the line. "Hey baby girl, what's going on?"

"I had a terrible day," I whimpered, tears filling my eyes for a moment. "I had a terrible fucking day and I'm so over it. I just want this week to be over. And I'm stressed and fucking all over the place because I'm a monster."

I could hear Daddy yelling in the background, but Papa's voice was smooth and relaxing. "I'm sorry, love. I know today sucked, but tomorrow will be better. You can come over for dinner this weekend if you want. I can talk Uncle Dracon into cooking something nice. Maybe bring this uh...mate you mentioned."

I fought off a smirk. "Well, maybe two."

"TWO!" Daddy howled in the background.

Papa snorted and I could imagine them right now—sitting in the kitchen, Daddy pacing back and forth like he always did when he was upset.

I heard a gruff bark from Ghost and sighed happily.

The idea of going home helped me relax a little, even though introducing Art and Calen to my family might be... a little insane.

"Speaking of," I said, "I need to go. They're cooking dinner for me. And I need to update them on some things at the office."

Such as how I'd most definitely banished Alice from the office in front of our teams, called and left a very heated voicemail to our big boss, and then typed up a very long and detailed email as well.

I wasn't playing anymore. I could cope with us merging companies. Hell, I could also cope with maybe losing my job. But, I couldn't deal with my team suffering at the hands of some unhinged HR rep.

"Okay, baby. I'll talk to you soon. If you need anything just let us know. We'll see you this weekend."

"Sounds good. I love you," I said, smiling.

"Love you too, baby. Bye."

We ended the call and I let out a little sigh, feeling some of the tension melt away.

Today had been shit but at least...

At least I was coming home to my mate.

My heart twisted some. Amidst all of the chaos, I had felt Art and Calen make a bond.

I wasn't mad about it.

In fact... I liked it.

I possibly liked Art a lot more than hated him.

I opened up my car door and slid out, grabbing my bag and then heading to the elevator that would take me up to my floor. I waited patiently, wishing that I was like Arthur and could just zap myself different places.

It took a few minutes, but I finally found myself on my floor and at my door. My keys jingled as I went to unlock it, but then the door flew open and I was met with Calen.

All of the troubles from earlier immediately melted away. "Hi," I said.

"Hi," he breathed, grinning.

Fuck, I felt everything light up around me at his warm smile. He stepped forward, giving me a hug and quick kiss.

"Mmm," I hummed, stepping inside and closing the door behind me. "Fuck, I think I needed that."

"I know," Calen said, kissing me on the lips this time.

Ah hell, he was too cute. He was way too cute, and all mine.

My apartment was warm and smelled like sex and pasta, a combination that I couldn't complain about. I glanced up at the kitchen, smirking at Art.

He was cooking, his back muscles rippling as he grilled chicken on the stove top. He looked back, arching a brow at me. "I take it all hell broke loose."

"It did," I sighed.

"Well we can eat first and then figure it out," Art said, surprising me.

"Let me get you wine," Calen said, pecking my cheek again.

I ruffled his hair before he stepped away, shrugging off my bag and then kicking off my heels. "I'm going to go change and then I'll join you both," I said.

"Sounds good," Art called.

I smirked a little as I moved towards my room, realizing quite happily that the chef was wearing nothing but an apron.

I could get used to this, I realized.

A little noise left my chest, almost a growl. I went to my room and changed, groaning as I unclasped my bra.

Calen's head poked through the doorway and I laughed. "Hey, such a perv," I teased.

"I just want to see what I'll be worshiping later, you know," Calen chuckled. "I was going to offer to help you undress and then give you wine."

"Hmmm, come here, witchling," I said. "You're too sweet for me."

Calen's eyes softened and he came to me, setting the glass of red wine on my side table first.

"How are you feeling now that you have two mates?" I asked, tipping up his chin.

Calen's eyes widened, his breath catching. "I hope it's okay. I should have talked to you first but—"

"Calen, it's fine," I said, giving him a soft growl. "I like Art, despite certain opinions of him prior to yesterday."

He let out a sigh of relief, leaning into me. "I feel better, more like myself. Less...sex crazed...although still definitely sex crazed."

"Good," I purred. "Maybe tonight we can completely break your heat."

"I don't know," Calen mumbled. "I've kind of liked all the attention."

"You'll still get all of our attention, you'll just be able to think a little clearer," I teased. "I'll still fuck you until you beg me to stop. You're mated to a succubus, my little witchling."

He grinned, sliding his hands up my stomach and then cupping one of my breasts. My tail flicked behind me, my blood heating.

"Dinner first for us, and then my dinner," I said.

"Okay," Calen mumbled, his eyes now on my boobs.

I smirked. "Grab me a shirt, will you?"

"I kind of like you naked..."

"Calen," I chuckled.

"Fine, fine," he said, shaking his head. I watched him snap himself out of boobie reverie and he went to my dresser, finding me a soft t-shirt.

I pulled it on, along with a pair of shorts, and sighed happily.

"Your wine, Mistress," Calen said, handing me the glass.

"Thank you, witchling," I said. "Let's go check on our chef."

The two of us went to the kitchen and I moved to my bar, taking a seat. Art turned for a second, winking at me.

"You look more relaxed and less likely to murder someone," Art teased.

"Mmm, well, I came home to a pretty boy to kiss, wine, food being made, and another pretty boy ass naked at the stove. It's hard to stay mad," I said, smirking.

Art snorted. "I'm making some fettuccine Alfredo with some garlic twists and a salad."

"Sounds amazing," I said, beaming. "Who knew Mr. Snakeroot was a chef?"

Calen chuckled, enjoying the banter between his two mates. He slid up next to me, taking the second bar seat.

My kitchen was set up perfectly for drinking wine and lounging while someone else cooked.

"Two minutes and we'll be ready," Art said. "You don't really have a dining room so I figured we'd eat at the bar."

"Yeah, I've been living the single life for awhile," I said.

"Same," Art and Calen both said.

The three of us laughed and I found myself finally shedding off the last bits of worry. We would all still need to talk about the plan for tomorrow, but…it could wait.

I was off the clock now, anyway.

Whatever happened at work could wait.

The oven started to go off and Calen was up again, grabbing an oven mitt and pulling out the pan of garlic knots. My mouth immediately watered, my stomach grumbling.

Feeding off sex fulfilled me the most, but I still liked eating food. Especially good food.

Art turned off the stove, giving the pasta a last mix with a spoon. He already had three plates ready to go and I fought the urge to get up and help.

He plated our food— pasta, salad, and bread. I hummed in my throat, ready to try the deliciousness he'd made.

"Bon Appetite," Art said, giving me a devilish grin as he set my plate down in front of me.

Calen handed me a napkin and a fork and then took the seat next to me again, letting out a cute little moan.

"I'm starving," he said. "I just realized I haven't been eating much."

I let out a low hiss, not pleased by that. I forgot that he needed to eat more than me.

"It's okay," he said quickly. "I'm fine, Inferna. I'm just hungry."

Art shook his head as he took the last barstool to my left, immediately digging into his pasta. "We've used a lot of magic too which is why we're both feeling it. Inferna, do you want to talk about what happened now?"

I let out a little sigh, and picked up my garlic knot. I bit into it, letting out a moan as I swallowed. "This is fucking good. And maybe," I sighed. "Long story short, I banished Alice."

Art nearly choked on his food and Calen made a noise, balking at me.

"Inferna," Art hissed. "You can't risk your job."

"Already at risk," I said, glaring off into space for a moment. "I wrote a very strongly worded email to the big boss. I basically told him to fuck off. I signed it off with Not so kind regards. I even called and it went straight to voicemail."

"Well, we at least have confirmation that Alice is crazy

and that something is going on," Art sighed. "Fuck. I don't want you to get fired."

I looked over at him, surprised by the genuine tone. I bit my lower lip for a moment, thinking. "If it happens, and you end up as the boss, then so be it. I can find another company to work for with my resume."

"There would be a huge turn over if you left," Art said. "That much is clear. Your team loves you."

"They do, which is why I did what I did today. Alice shouldn't be immune to consequences just because of the position she is in. And the people we work for shouldn't be unreachable. I don't know what happened when they merged Warts and Claws, but the company will just go straight downhill if this is how it ends up. It's bullshit. Also," I growled, "I may have threatened her rather loudly in front of everyone. Really, that's the only thing I can think of that will get me fired."

"Well," Art said, shaking his head. "I can't say I would have reacted differently. If you hadn't told me to take Calen, then... I would have kicked her out too."

"She should be thankful," I muttered, twisting up a bite of pasta onto my fork. "I let her walk out alive. Calen, are you okay from that? What was she doing?"

"I can't remember," Calen admitted, "She was using magic to try and break into my mind, but I don't know why."

I didn't like that answer.

"Is there anything special about your family? I mean, it seems like omega witches are rare, according to both of you. Could this be some sort of attack?" I asked.

"They're rare but not that rare," Calen said. "And I think that our case was just special given that I had both of you around at the same time and...I don't know. My family is quiet and doesn't have any bad history."

"All witches have bad history," I said. "Same for monsters. All of us have some skeletons in the closet. Hell, I know one of my dads has murdered people. He's been around for ages too. Speaking of, I would like to take the two of you to meet my family this weekend. If that's okay."

Both Art and Calen choked on their food this time, coughing. I narrowed my eyes, trying not to laugh as they pounded their chests and cleared their throats.

"Meeting your family?" Art rasped.

"Here, sweetheart, have some wine," I said, giving him my glass.

Art actually took a sip, washing down whatever reservations he had. "Fucking hell, I don't know. What if they hate me?"

"Well, one of them will hate both of you, but it's fine. He'll get over it. The other one will adore both of you. So long as Ghost approves, then we'll be good," I said, grinning.

"Who is Ghost?" Calen asked, his voice having just a hint of fear.

"Our family dog that's been around longer than I have," I laughed. "Don't worry. It'll be fine. I do have a big family."

Did I tell them now about how many uncles I had or did I wait?

"It'll be fine," I said.

"Every time you say that, I believe you less," Art teased, shaking his head. "Well, I guess that means you should mate me then."

It was my turn to almost choke, and it was echoed by Calen's laugh.

"Here I was thinking that I'm blunt," I said, stealing my

wine glass away from him. I took a sip, mulling it over. "Is that an offer, Mr. Snakeroot?"

"One that I hope you can't resist," he said, giving me a charming grin.

I narrowed my gaze on him, studying him. He was still ass naked aside from the apron, his dark hair and beard disheveled. He wasn't prim and proper, but kind of...kind of a dork. A cute one. One that I wanted to devour.

"Perhaps you should feed your body first," I said, looking down at his plate.

"Yeah, and then you can feed off our bodies," Calen teased.

"Mmm, finish your food, witchling," I said, already thinking about exactly what I wanted to do to the two of them.

We did have Calen's heat to break, after all.

CHAPTER FOURTEEN
sex magic

ART

Inferna pushed me back onto the bed, straddling my hips. My cock was hard and I was already naked, my blood humming with magic.

She licked her lips, her forked tongue flicking over her fangs.

Calen was sitting at the head of the bed, watching us while he stroked his own cock.

After dinner, Inferna had made it clear that it was time.

Either, I submitted to her and we mated or...

Well, I wasn't sure what the 'or' was because I said yes.

It was insane but I didn't care. I knew this was right, and despite how much I'd hated her yesterday morning— I'd had a change of heart.

The sound of Calen stroking himself made me moan and I looked over at our little mate. His cheeks were flushed, his golden eyes blazing with lust.

"Look at me," Inferna said, the tip of her tail pushing my face.

I looked up at her, swallowing hard.

I was so used to being the one in control. But, not with her.

I liked submitting to her.

"And here I was thinking that we hated each other," Inferna said, the tip of her crimson tail tracing down my chest.

My heart pounded, a little moan leaving me. "I want you," I rasped.

I sounded so fucking desperate.

But, I was. I wanted to fill her over and over again, to feel her lock my cock inside of her.

I watched in awe as she pulled her shirt over her head, her breasts now free. I sat up immediately, capturing one of her nipples between my lips.

She cradled my head, rubbing her pussy against my hard cock. "Good boy," she purred. "Mmm, that feels good."

Fucking hell, she was going to drive me crazy. Everything about her was perfect. I sucked her nipple, playing with it with my tongue and teeth while I started to play with her other.

She let out a feminine chuckle, one that made me shiver against her.

I was her plaything. Her toy. Boss or not, outside of the office she dominated me.

"So submissive," she whispered. "Are you certain you want this, Art?"

I pulled away for a moment, resting my chin between her breasts as I looked up at her. "I think I know what I want. I always have and always will. I'm a leader at work for a reason, Mistress."

"True, but mating a succubus is a little different than charts and managing people," she said, arching a dark brow.

Fuck, she was gorgeous. She was smart and cunning and... "Inferna, I want you as much as I want Calen. Do you want me?"

"Yes," she said, smirking. "If I didn't want you, you wouldn't be hard beneath me right now while playing with me."

"So can we stop asking if we're all sure we want this? I think we've all agreed to this little merger," I said, grinning.

Inferna shoved me back onto the mattress again, the blankets poofing up around us. "Yes, sir, I think we all agree."

Just hearing her say sir almost made me cum all over her. Calen made a little noise, his breath hitching.

"Don't worry about our witchling right now," Inferna instructed. "He's hard and needy but he likes watching us. He wants to see me take your hard monstrous cock."

"Fuck," I whispered, closing my eyes for a moment of pure pleasure as she slid down my body, gripping me.

The tip of her tongue flicked over the head, making me gasp.

"So sensitive," she murmured. "I bet I could make you cum just by licking up your precum."

"Mistress," I begged. "Please let me fuck you."

"No," she said. "Not yet. You're going to lie there like a good boy and let me play with your pretty cock. And then when I'm ready, I'll let you bury yourself inside of me."

"Thank you," I whispered. "Thank you."

Another cry left me as she took my cock into her mouth, sucking me. She moved her hand up and down, her mouth finding the same rhythm.

She was taking her time, her movements slow enough to make me feel desperate and crazed.

"Mistress," I rasped. "Please."

She pulled her lips from me, licking them as she met my gaze. My body had a light sheen to it now, my magic becoming stronger and stronger. We were feeding off each other, I realized.

She fed off sexual energy and that energy we created in turn gave me stronger magic.

"You're so pretty when you glow," she said, smirking. "I like that about you, witch. You're like a little star."

I made a noise, a groan and a growl together. She continued to stroke me, edging me until I was about to cum.

She pulled her hand away, sliding off me to the side.

I immediately sat up, knowing what she wanted. What I wanted. I rolled over, pulling her body beneath me. Her legs wrapped around my hips, her body moving beneath me.

Our lips met in a hungry kiss, one that would be burned into my mind forever. I drank her in— her taste, her scent, the feel of her body beneath me.

Her nails raked down my back, making me gasp. She leaned up, her lips brushing over my ear.

"Give me all you have," she commanded.

"Yes, Mistress," I breathed.

She was so wet. So fucking wet and ready for me. I looked down between us, moaning at the sight of my cock rubbing against her fanged entrance.

"The teeth," I rasped.

"They'll feel good," she promised.

Fuck, she was right.

I started to ease inside of her, groaning as the fangs dragged over my cock. If there was any pain, it was immediately replaced by wave after wave of pleasure.

She was so hot, so fucking tight. Fuck, she was mine.

"I said give me all you have, not be gentle," she growled.

"Fuck," I cursed.

With that, I thrust inside of her— her cry driving me insane. I felt the worries and gentle edge melt away, replaced by my desire to breed her. To fuck her as hard as I could, to make her cum around me.

"Goddess, you feel good," I gasped.

Inferna only moaned, her head tipping back. I gripped her thighs and began to pump in and out, gasping as our magic became even stronger.

It was addicting. Thrilling. The lust and desires that we had were melting together, creating a blanket of pure ecstasy around us. I thrust in and out, watching her take every fucking inch.

"Harder," she gasped.

I growled, gripping her thighs harder. Calen's moan melted into ours as he watched me fuck her. Every movement was given with all the strength I had, her body moving beneath me with each thrust.

"Fuck," I gasped. "Fuck, I'm going to cum."

"Not until you make me," she moaned.

I slid my hand down, my thumb finding her clit. I started to rub it in circles while I pumped in and out, and watched as she went wild beneath me.

I had to make her cum. I wanted to see her release, to feel her squeeze around me right before I came inside of her.

"Cum for me, Mistress," I gasped.

She moaned, her body bowing up beneath me. I pumped into her harder, circling her clit faster and faster.

She growled, her fangs glinting. I reached down, twisting one of her nipples.

This time, she screamed and I felt her start to cum.

"Fuck," I snarled, lost in how gorgeous she was. Lost in how it felt to watch her release, to feel her cumming around me.

I was going to lose it. I couldn't stop myself. With another couple of thrusts, I felt my knot slip inside of her— spreading her wide— and then I felt the teeth clamp around me, locking us in place.

I started to orgasm, my hot cum shooting inside of her. Inferna groaned, melting beneath me as I filled her up, our bodies humming together like two heated engines.

We were both panting as I leaned down, giving her a soft kiss. She wrapped her arms around my neck, letting out a little moan. "Speak your spell, witch," she whispered.

I felt it on the tip of my tongue and didn't stop it, letting it roll off freely. I felt the zap of the magic we'd created, the initial sting turning into an entirely new type of pleasure as a bond rooted between our souls.

We both moaned, holding on to each other tightly.

"I'm yours," I whispered, tears burning my eyes.

Fuck, I wasn't just with one— I had two mates.

After years of being alone, of having no family, I couldn't find a shred of regret about taking Inferna and Calen.

I was theirs.

"You're mine," Inferna agreed, nuzzling me. "I can feel sadness from you. Are you okay?"

"I'm okay," I whispered, melting against her.

"Overwhelmed?" she asked, stroking me.

"Maybe a little," I admitted, barely above a whisper.

I felt Calen responding too, our bonds echoing with soft energy. With love and kindness.

"Come here, witchling," Inferna murmured. "Come cuddle us."

I turned my face over, watching Calen crawl over to us. He gave me a sweet kiss before settling down next to Inferna, his arms wrapping around the two of us.

"Just rest," Inferna said gently. "Tomorrow will be an interesting day. But, at least we won't have to handle it alone."

True.

"In fact, I don't think the three of us will ever have to handle anything alone again."

I made a noise, feeling my heart ache.

I had been alone for a very long time and it was uncomfortable to think of relying on others. But...

It also felt good. It felt like magic, the kind that was used to heal.

"Go to sleep, my witches. I love you both."

I already felt myself drifting to sleep and didn't fight it, allowing the wave to drag me into good dreams.

CHAPTER FIFTEEN
hump day

CALEN

I set my backpack down on my desk and let out a sigh. A happy sigh, despite all of the weird looks I was getting.

"Hey," I said, greeting Lora, Hazard, and the manticore who still hadn't given me his name.

Lora gave me a little smile. "You look much better, Calen."

"Thanks," I said, sitting down in my chair. "Feeling much better."

It was true. This morning, I had woken up between Inferna and Art. The three of us had fucked each other slowly, and then I'd showered and dressed— coming straight here.

We'd even carpooled, despite the fact that there would most definitely be speculation soon.

Hazard grinned like an idiot and was about to say something, when a throat was cleared next to us.

Our table looked up, surprised to see Sally.

I didn't like Sally and the feeling was mutual.

Hell, most people didn't like Sally. She'd been the secretary for Art for a long time and she was efficient, but she was very two faced.

"I ran the reports per our bosses' direction and the four of you really need to focus on getting more done. You did less tasks than everyone else yesterday," Sally snipped.

"Yesterday wasn't a normal day," Lora protested, glaring. "Who the fuck are you?"

"I'm the assistant manager," Sally sneered.

"Like hell you are," Hazard snapped. "What the hell are you talking about, Sally? There are no assistant managers."

"Yes. They gave me that title once they merged the company," Sally said, glaring at us. "And you, Mich, you in particular need to work on your quality."

The manticore, who was named Mich, slowly pulled off his headphones. I leaned back, looking between the monster and back to Sally.

"I think you should leave before I gut you, Sally," Mich said, his tone deceptively polite. "I'd hate to see you end up like our HR rep."

Sally gasped, her ears turning red. "That HR rep will be back, just you watch. They'll fire Inferna and Arthur and then I'll be in charge. Then, I'll fire your lazy ass."

"Sally," I snapped, interjecting. "Leave us alone. No one here likes you and unless you want to do all the bug tasks yourself, you should leave us alone."

Sally scoffed, her eyes narrowing in on me. "You little slut. You think you're all good and secure because you sleep with the boss—"

A pair of scissors went flying, narrowly missing Sally's face. She screamed, looking at Mich like he was the devil.

I glanced back at him, surprised that he'd just done that. The scissors were now buried deep in a pole behind her.

"Go away," Hazard growled. "You're fucking with our vibes."

"Leave," he snarled.

"Get out before I make you dance for an eternity," Lora sneered.

Sally scoffed, pointing a shaky finger at me. "Slut."

With that, she marched off.

"What a bitch," Mich sighed, grabbing his headphones.

"What the fuck was that?" I asked, shaking my head.

"Sounds like she's jealous you're getting dick and she's not," Lora said.

"Hey," I said, "I'm not—"

All three of them hit me with knowing looks and flat expressions.

"Monsters can smell better than witches," Mich said, fighting off a feline smirk. "I think you should save yourself the trouble and not lie, witch. We're fine with it over here, especially since you were the reason that HR bitch got kicked out. She's lucky she didn't die. Inferna definitely has a temper."

I rubbed the back of my head, not sure how to respond. If we were just humans, it would be easy to lie about Inferna, Art, and me. But, I knew that Hazard could see our auras and I knew that Mich and Lora could smell that they were my mates.

Fuck, we hadn't thought this through.

"Also," Lora said. "We really don't have much work to do. It's only 9:15 and I think we can get most of this done by 10 a.m. But then, we should have a little fun."

I arched a brow and all three of us leaned in, intrigued by what the little pixie demon had to say.

She grinned, flashing her pearly white fangs.

"I like having fun," Hazard said, smirking. "I think we could have fun with Sally in particular. Never liked her anyway. And I know where she keeps her things."

"I don't like bullying people," Mich said, "but I can make an exception."

"Great," Lora said. "Let me see if I can get a couple people in on it. I know Anne doesn't like her at all."

"Awesome," I said, smirking.

I felt my phone go off in my pocket and drew it out, glancing at the text message.

Art: I'm going to knot you on my desk at lunch. Inferna wants to watch.

Fuck. I swallowed hard and then flushed red at the sound of Mich whistling.

"Oh boy," he chuckled next to me.

"Hey," I said, pulling my phone out of sight.

Mich snorted and put his headphones back on.

It was almost comical to watch him work on a computer — a massive muscled manticore just typing away. I shook my head, glancing at the text again.

Another one popped up, this time from Inferna.

Inferna: Don't get hard thinking about Art breeding you over and over again

Fucking hell. I felt my cock stir and scooted in closer, making sure that the desktop covered me.

They were going to torture me like this.

I let out a little hiss and opened my phone screen, creating a group chat with the two of them really quickly.

> Hey, I'm trying to work!!!

Inferna: Awww yeah. Let me ask your boss if it's okay for you to get fucked later for lunch. Hey, Art?
Art: Yes, Mistress?
Inferna: Can Calen be fucked and bred by you later? Can he get hard and needy just thinking about it? Trying to hide it from his co-workers
Art: Yes, he can. Of course

> Both of you are asses

That was responded with a bunch of laughing emojis from Art and then one devil one from Inferna.

Inferna: Watch your tongue, witchling

I let out a sigh, sitting back in my seat.

> Yes, Mistress.

I closed my phone, focusing on my desk.
I felt someone watching me and looked up, seeing Sally hawk eyeing us from across the room.
"Fuck, she's weird," I mumbled, looking away.
"She is," Lora agreed. "Alright, boys, let's get to work."

WE KNOCKED OUT OUR WORK QUICKLY AND I FOUND that working with Lora and Mich actually made things easier. The four of us were able to do things much faster together— and the other groups seemed to be experiencing the same thing.

So far, there had only been a couple of hiccups. A couple of the monsters didn't like a couple of the witches, but at least my group was good.

"Lunch time," Mich said, standing up with a soft roar. "I'm gonna eat them out again."

Lora giggled, standing up too. "Hazard and Calen, you both coming?"

"I...can't," I said, wincing a little.

Hazard, Lora, and Mich laughed. "Fine," Hazard chuckled. "But yes, I'll join you creatures. Let's see if we can steal extra dessert."

The three of them left, heading for the elevators.

I sat still for a couple of minutes, waiting for others to leave as I pretended to work.

My phone went off, the screen lighting up.

Inferna: To the office. Now.

Fuck. I stood up immediately, locking my computer screen and then grabbing my phone. I headed across the floor to their office, stepping through the doorway.

They were both at their desks, busy typing away.

"Put up a wall of magic so they can't see," Art instructed.

I squinted, unsure of what they were planning. Still, I obeyed and used my magic to shield us from prying eyes. The doorway took on a shimmering green curtain, giving us some privacy.

Suddenly, they seemed to be working together quite well. It was both thrilling and a little scary, like two evil masterminds falling in love.

"By the way, Sally was being a bitch earlier and saying she's the assistant manager," I said, looking from Inferna to Art.

Art scowled. "What?"

"Yes. And also my group has figured out the three of us are sleeping together."

Inferna snorted and Art scowled even more.

"Well, it was bound to happen. You smell like us now, Calen," Inferna said, shrugging.

"It could create problems," Art sighed.

"It could, but I doubt it," Inferna said. "I've already seen some of the monsters eyeing some of the witches. I would be surprised if no one else violates Alice's little HR policies. Speaking of," Inferna said, looking straight at me. "Strip."

Her command made me groan a little. I felt my cock immediately harden and I stepped to the center of the office, starting with the buttons of my shirt. I popped them open slowly, working down the shirt. I let it fall to the floor, and then tossed my undershirt there too.

Inferna leaned back in her chair, twirling a pen like a baton between her fingers as she watched me with her black eyes. She was wearing a black dress today, one that hugged her figure and made me want to worship her. She had shrugged her blazer off and it draped behind her, her lips drawn into a red smirk.

"What do you think of our witchling, Art?" Inferna asked.

"I think I want him to take off his pants."

I smiled to myself now. I unbuckled my belt and then unbuttoned my pants, kicking them off.

"And his boxers."

My cock was hard as I stripped them off, leaving me completely exposed to my bosses.

To my mates.

I could feel their lust through the bonds, how much they both wanted me. I could feel the wickedness and...

"Go to Art's desk," Inferna said. "I'm going to instruct the two of you on what to do."

"Yes, Mistress," I whispered.

I went to his desk, looking straight at him. He was lounging in his seat, the air of mischief making us both smile.

"Hi, Boss," I said, winking at him.

His eyes darkened, his smile faltering as a cloud of lust overtook him.

"Take the ruler from your desk," Inferna said.

Art opened the top drawer, drawing out a metal ruler.

Fuck.

"Oh, and the sharpie."

Art obeyed, pulling out one of the permanent markers.

"Bend over the desktop, witchling."

"Yes, Mistress," I whispered.

I leaned over the desk, the cold of the wood making me shiver. I let out a little groan, my cock hard and throbbing.

"I want you to write 'property of Inferna' on his ass," Inferna said.

"Yes, Mistress," Art said, walking around behind me.

I heard the cap click as he pulled it off, the felt tip dragging across my skin as he wrote.

Fuck, that was hot.

I was already hers and his, but having that written on me...

Being branded and then spanked...

I bit my lower lip, letting out a little groan. Art finished writing, taking a step back.

"Take a picture of his ass before and then we'll take one after."

Art moved around his desk, grabbing his phone. I moaned as he came back around, snapping a picture of me bent over his desk— 'property of Inferna' written over my ass.

"Good," Inferna chuckled. "Such good, obedient boys."

"Mistress," I moaned, desperate.

"Now, grab the ruler and spank him however you wish."

Fuck. Art chuckled as he leaned over, pausing to give me a kiss on the lips before plucking the ruler from his desk. I groaned as he stood behind me again, tracing the chilled metal across my skin.

"You look so good bent over my desk and desperate to be fucked," Art said softly.

"Fuck," I rasped.

He chuckled and I felt the anticipation, holding my breath.

"No, no," Inferna corrected. "Breathe while he spanks you. And remember your safeword."

I let out the breath, groaning. "Yes, Mistress."

Art waited for me to let out an audible breath and then he began to pat my ass, warming up my skin. It was quicker than last time, his firm hand smacking me quickly.

The first slap of the ruler had me hissing and I cried out, groaning.

"Ohhh," Inferna purred. "Fuck, you're right, Art. He does make cute little screams."

Fuck. I moaned, thrusting my hips a little so I could rub my cock over the desktop.

"See," Art said. "He does like a little pain."

"I do," I agreed, gritting my teeth.

Art struck me again, the sting making me wince while

also making me harder. I sucked in a breath, gripping the edges of the desk.

Thwap, thwap, thwap.

Three hits, each one more intense than the last. I gasped and cried, "FUCK!"

Art growled, tossing the ruler to the floor. He moved to spread my ass when he froze.

Inferna got up immediately, cursing under her breath.

"What's wrong?" I asked.

"We have company," Inferna growled. "Fucking hell. I will stall them."

"Who?" I asked, feeling a stab of panic.

Art was already grabbing my clothes, cursing under his breath. "Fuck, there's no way I can hide this hard on. Or Calen's."

Inferna hissed under her breath. "You two make each other cum then, but use the best magic you have to hide. I can keep them out until you're done. Calen, I want you to go home sick after this. They won't be able to sense as much between Art and me."

Before I could answer, Inferna pulled on her blazer and headed out of the office, leaving the two of us behind.

CHAPTER SIXTEEN
pranks and pens

INFERNA

"Claude," I said, using the most calming and seductive tone I could muster. "I didn't expect you here, considering I haven't received any responses to any of my emails."

Claude, the owner of Claws and now partial owner of Warts & Claws Inc., was standing in the office kitchenette. He was an ominous vampire, one that had a sleek aura of power I admired.

I'd never had any issues with Claude until this week. And hell, I knew his history too. He had always been a somewhat decent blood sucker.

"Inferna," Claude said, crossing his arms. "I saw your email. I came to investigate. I've never received such a harsh email from you before. And I have no idea what you're talking about."

"What do you mean?" I asked, tilting my head.

We studied each other and it felt like I had just sat

down at a chess game. Claude wore a nice suit, one that cost more than my car. It was navy blue with silver cufflinks, and a soft silk shirt underneath. He had icy blonde hair, eyes that were a deep green with red flecks, and he was just a little taller than me.

No one else was on the floor now aside from him and me— and then Art and Calen.

"Where is everyone?" Claude asked.

"At lunch. What is gong on, Claude?"

Claude's expression flickered for a moment and he pressed his lips together. "Where is Alice?"

One question for another.

"Perhaps we should take a seat," I said, gesturing at the table.

"Behind closed doors would probably be better, but I'm guessing the two in the other office are busy."

Fuck.

Claude gave me a faint smile. "I'm quite old, Inferna, and I'm not very stupid."

"Of course you're not stupid," I said. "And neither am I. Alice isn't here. Alice attacked one of my employees yesterday. Alice created a disruption in the workplace with her attitude and I handled it not as well as I could have."

"Right," Claude chuckled, relaxing just a little. "I appreciate your bluntness."

"And I don't appreciate you being vague."

"Claude," a voice chirped.

Goddamn it. Damn it all to hell.

I turned around, somehow not surprised to see none other than Alice.

"She is not welcome in this office," I said, looking back at Claude.

His eyes had changed, his posture going from relaxed to...robotic?

I scowled, looking from him back to her.

Alice arched a brow. "I told you I would be back. You're getting fired today Inferna, you and your fucking pet."

"You'll have to be more specific," I said. "As to whom you are referring as my 'fucking pet'. As a succubus, I have many of those."

Alice hissed, glaring. "That omega witch."

"Omega witch?" Claude asked. "You mean we found him?"

"*Claude*," Alice hissed.

Fuck, I didn't like the sound of that.

I took a step back, looking directly at him. "Claude. What is this about?"

Claude's gaze flickered again, his expression wavering.

I wasn't a witch so I couldn't see magic, but I wasn't a dumbass. Something was affecting him.

I mentally reached out to Calen and Art, tugging on our bonds.

Calen, leave and go to my home. Don't let anyone in.

What? I felt him respond.

I could feel Art too, his worry and confusion.

There was something else going on. I may not have been an ancient creature like Claude, but I could feel it. I trusted my instincts even when it felt like I could be wrong.

"Where is dear Calen?" Alice asked sweetly.

"Home," I said. "He is home sick for the day."

"And yet, I can smell him on you," Alice sneered.

Fuck this job. A low growl left me, my fangs bared. "If you want to die today, I'll stake you with every fucking pen in this office."

"That's a good way to get fired," Alice snapped.

"That's a good way to make sure you're dead, too," I snipped.

"Inferna," Claude said firmly. "We need the omega witch."

"Why?" I asked, my voice loud.

I knew that any moment, people would start to come back from lunch.

I needed that, needed the moment of distraction.

"No one will leave this building," Alice said. "No one will leave this building until we are done."

"What do we have here?"

I turned, thankful to see Art. He came up behind me, our gazes locking for a split second.

"You must be Claude," Art said smoothly, looking at the vampire boss. "I've heard wonderful things about you."

"Have you?" Claude asked drily, holding out his hand.

Art took it, giving it a firm shake.

"I have. I've heard about your family," Art said.

"I've heard about yours."

Art immediately stiffened, his jaw setting.

"Hmm. I didn't say that I have family," Art said, stepping back.

It was us against them. If we fought, would we be able to handle two vampires?

"And what of Alex?" Art asked. "Is he joining us today, or is it just you two?"

"Alex," Alice sneered, "Is busy."

"Excellent. Well, we will wait until he is not busy to continue this meeting. It feels a little unprofessional and—ah, I hear our employees returning from lunch," Art said, grinning.

Alice started to protest but Claude hissed at her, silencing her. As if on cue, different groups started coming back— all giving us looks once they realized Alice was here.

"Hey, I thought you banished her." Poppins growled, pointing at Alice.

"Yeah," Lora said, crossing her arms. "She freaking tried to break into my mind yesterday."

Claude's brows shot up and he cleared his throat. "We will return tomorrow, with Alex. We will settle things then."

Before I could answer, the witch receptionist came marching up to our group— fuming.

"THEY PUT MY PENS IN PUDDING!" Sally screeched, pointing at Lora, Mich, and one of the Warts witches.

"We did not," the witch called, but his lips were quivering as he fought off a grin.

"THEY PUT MY PENS IN PUDDING! I WANT THEM FIRED!" Sally screamed. "This is unacceptable."

"Sally," Art barked, silencing her. "You screaming is unacceptable. What has gotten into you?"

Sally jabbed a finger at Alice. "Fire them. That's what you're here for, right?"

What the hell was happening to our office?

Alice hissed, shaking her head. "Claude and I are leaving. I will see you both tomorrow."

Sally scoffed as Claude and Alice passed by her, heading past everyone that had just come back from lunch.

Sally turned her furious gaze on me, marching straight up to me. The idiot raised her hand, pointing a finger at me.

"You bitch. This is all your fault!"

Before I could snap back, all of the lights in the room went out and Art stepped in front of me— his skin glowing bright blue.

"You dare speak to her that way?" Art growled.

Fucking hell.

"Art," I said softly. "It's okay."

Art's magic snapped in angry wisps around him and Sally took a step back, her eyes wide.

"I told you, the cards said she would be bad for you! All of us are doomed! All of you!" Sally yelled.

"Get the fuck out of my building," Art growled. "Before I speak a spell that will leave your tongue on the floor."

"I was such a good receptionist!" Sally shrieked.

"GET. OUT. NOW!" Art thundered.

Sally scurried away, heading straight for the elevators.

I put my hand on his shoulder, pushing calming vibes through our link. He let out a breath, his chest heaving. He turned to look at me, even though we were being watched by everyone.

"We need to call a meeting," I whispered. "But we can't do that in the dark, love."

Art let out a frustrated growl, but the dark edge of his magic began to disperse. The lights flickered and then came back on, lighting up all of the surprised faces of our teams.

"Meeting time!" Art barked, looking at everyone. "Five minutes, team."

"We're going to figure out what's going on," I said, giving a reassuring nod to everyone.

One way or another.

CHAPTER SEVENTEEN
boss

ART

"Are we all going to get fired?"

I looked around the room, meeting the gaze of Poppins — one of the Claws creatures. He was a nice griffin, the one I'd met in the elevator.

"No," I said. "No one is getting fired. Well, at least none of you."

"What the hell is going on?" Hazard asked, shaking his head.

"I don't know," I answered, "But, it's not right and it's not normal."

"I think that they're out to get Calen," Inferna said, looking around the room.

The two of us were side by side, handling a round table discussion with everyone on our team. A total of 25 faces looked back at us, a combination of creatures and witches.

"Your mate," one of the creatures grumbled.

No one could feel Inferna stiffen except for me, and that was only because of our bond that we shared.

"Yes. There has been a romance this week. Calen is now my mate, as is Arthur. It does technically violate the rules," Inferna answered bluntly.

"No one cares," Lora chimed, shrugging. "So long as he isn't treated differently. I think all of us are adults. Not only that, most of us here understand how mates work."

"Well," I said, feeling my cheeks heat up some. "It was unexpected."

A couple of the witches from my team snorted and I narrowed my eyes. One of them, an elemental witch named Clay, raised his hands.

"All of us on our team know you and Calen have been a thing," Clay said.

I sighed, rubbing my eyes for a moment.

"It's great," Inferna glossed over. "It's fine. Office romances happen. Also, I'm pretty certain Alice is going to fire me so…"

"If you're fired, then I'm leaving," Poppins announced loudly. "But also, what the hell is happening with these evil plans? Alice straight up tried to steal thoughts from Lora. Then she trapped Calen."

"Why?" Hazard asked, echoing the question everyone had.

"I don't know," Inferna admitted. "I don't know. It's unclear. But, maybe tomorrow we'll get some answers. Either way, I want all of you to know that I've enjoyed working with you."

"Hold on," I said, looking over at Inferna. "Inferna, you're still the boss. We don't know that you won't be at the end of this week."

"I banished our HR rep and then damn near ripped into Claude, the guy that owns our side of the company."

"Well," I said, wincing. "It'll work out. You're still the boss."

"You'll always be our boss," one of the creatures said.

I really needed to learn everyone's names at some point.

Well, unless I was fired too.

There was a murmur of agreement and Inferna made a little noise. I could feel the echo of sadness from her, which made me worry.

She felt a lot more for her team than I did, I realized. Not that I didn't like my team, but she loved hers.

"I don't know much," Clay said, glancing around at everyone, "but there have been rumors on the underside of our...society. About a witch-hunt from certain creatures. But they're after only certain types of witches."

I arched a brow, crossing my arms. "Really?"

"Yeah," Clay said, pressing his lips together. "I don't know what type of witches. But if Calen is an omega then maybe that's part of it."

Perhaps. My jaw stiffened and I stole a glance at Inferna, who shared the same expression I did. A mask, one that was calm while on the inside we were both panicking.

I had grown up around the dark corners of the witch world. The coven I had been born into had been a dark one, where most of the elders had sacrificed themselves to bring a creature back. I still didn't know all the details, but the magic I had known had always been dark.

Which was why it had been good of Inferna to interrupt me when I'd nearly lost my temper on Sally. I was still cooling down from it too, my entire body on edge.

This week had been a rollercoaster.

"Do you have anyone you know that can give more info on that?" I asked.

Clay shook his head, scowling. "No. Sorry."

"No worries," Inferna glazed over, despite how worried we both were.

"What about your family, Inferna?" Anne asked. "Could they help?"

"Of course they could," Inferna sighed. "We'll see, I was taught how to handle things pretty well on my own."

I still didn't know much about her family, but now I wondered.

"Alright," I said, clearing my throat. "We only have a couple hours left in the day. I'm going to go try and get ahold of Alex. I'm starting to wonder if the witch is even alive. If anyone needs anything, just call Inferna or me."

Everyone nodded and with that, our meeting dispersed.

Inferna and I went back to our office and I shut the door carefully behind me.

Inferna stood still for a few moments and I went up behind her, circling my arms around her and resting my chin on her shoulder.

"You're a good boss," I whispered.

She made a little noise and turned, burying her face against my chest. I held her, wondering how I had become trusted enough for this very strong woman to let herself break just a little in front of me.

"I'm worried," she murmured.

I nodded, holding her a little tighter. "There are darker things at work here and I don't know how it ended up happening, but I'm thankful to have you and Calen."

"Is Calen safe?" she whispered.

"I think so," I said, rubbing her back. I felt the ridges around her shoulder blades where her wings stayed hidden unless she fully shifted, gliding my hand up to the back of her neck.

I gave her a gentle squeeze, wishing that I could cast a curse on Alice and Claude.

"I'm going to reach out to one of my vampire friends and perhaps a couple of other creatures. I don't know how we're supposed to expect people to still work if this is how it is."

"I don't either," I said. "But, at least we know both of our teams have our back. Aside from Sally."

Inferna gave a soft chuckle. "I thought you were going to turn her into a gerbil."

"You did not," I hissed, fighting off a grin. "For fuck's sake, I'm not that barbaric."

"I don't know," Inferna teased. I felt the tip of her tail trace up the back of my thigh. "You were kind of hot in the way you took control. I kind of liked it."

"Did you?" I asked, feeling my cock harden.

"Yeah," she said, her hand sliding up my chest.

She gripped my tie, pulling me into a kiss. Our lips met and I groaned, drinking in her taste and scent.

I broke away for a moment, my breaths coming in pants. "Do we have time for a quickie before we seek to destroy our bosses?"

"Always time for a quickie," Inferna said, "Fuck me hard, Boss."

"Fuck," I growled.

I gripped her hips, walking her back as our lips met again. She groaned, still gripping my tie as I lifted her and seated her on her desktop.

Fuck, she was perfect. Her tail still traced the back of my thigh, moving up my ass to my waistband.

"Inferna," I groaned. "Fuck."

She kissed up my jaw, running her sharp nails through my beard and up to my hair. She gripped me, pulling my head to the side and she nipped my earlobe.

I was so hard now. So fucking hard. And somehow, even though she was letting me lead— I knew she was the one in control.

I kissed down her neck, unbuttoning her blazer and then pushing it off. I paused, admiring the curve of her shoulders and how her dress dipped. I looked down, moaning.

"A goddess," I whispered, pushing the shoulder straps of her dress down. I pushed her bra straps to the side too, running the back of my knuckles down to her breast. "A sexy, stunning, smart goddess. I don't know how you're mine," I murmured.

Inferna moaned as I circled one of her nipples with my thumb, enjoying the way they both perked. I leaned down, taking one between my teeth.

"Ah, fuck, Art," she gasped.

I bit her and then sucked, rolling it with my tongue. Her nails raked over my shoulders, the tip of her tail moving around to my cock. I reached down and undid my belt quickly, unzipping my pants.

Her tail immediately slipped in, rubbing against me. I groaned, sucking her harder before alternating to her other breast. She moaned, tipping her head back.

I growled, pushing her back on the desk. Office supplies flew, falling off onto the floor as I hiked up her dress.

She was stunning.

"I want you to cum on my mouth so that I can taste you for the rest of the day," I rasped..

Inferna spread her legs for me and I bit my bottom lip. She was wearing a black lace thong, one that I wanted to rip with my teeth. I leaned down, running my tongue over her clit.

"*Witch*," she groaned.

I grinned against her, gripping her thighs. My blood hummed with magic and I whispered a spell, one that made my fingertips feel almost electric.

Inferna gasped, bowing against me. "Fuck, I didn't know you could do that."

"There's a lot I can do," I chuckled, burying my face against her pussy again.

Inferna groaned, her nails dragging over the desktop. I ran my fingers across her, enjoying the way my magic crackled over her red skin.

I ran my tongue over the lace, breathing in her scent as her hips bucked against me.

She needed release. I could feel how badly she needed to cum.

Fuck, I was her slave. I was her pet.

I was her mate.

"Art," she growled.

I moved the strip of lace to the side, immediately circling her clit with my tongue. I slid two fingers inside of her, moaning.

She was so wet for me, so needy.

The teeth around her opening scraped lightly across my skin as I began to work my fingers in and out of her, flicking and sucking her clit. Her back bowed up, her gasps becoming closer and closer together.

She was going to let me make her cum, and that was a gift.

"I'm so close," she rasped.

I growled against her, increasing the rhythm. My cock was hard in my pants, my body thrumming with the energy we created. My skin cast a soft glow on her as she cried out. I felt the fangs close in as her muscles restricted and she came hard, her scream music to my ears.

I leaned down, lapping up her cum. She tasted like heaven, her cum covering my chin.

I would smell and taste her all day until I got to share her again with Calen.

I sat back, rubbing her thighs. "You're perfect," I whispered.

She gave a little helpless moan and I grinned.

"I kind of like seeing you like this," I chuckled.

She raised her head, her black eyes piercing me. "I'm still your Mistress."

"You are still the boss," I chuckled.

Only a couple more hours and then we'd go home to our mate.

CHAPTER EIGHTEEN
almost friday

CALEN

I stood on the sidewalk, looking up at my building. It was Thursday, and I had woken up this morning between my two mates.

I'd almost forgotten I still had my own apartment. It was a good thing I didn't have any pets or plants, because I wasn't sure I would have remembered them through the whirlwind of this week.

Still, I needed to grab some of my things.

Last night, the three of us had relaxed and watched movies until falling asleep. I'd learned that Art had a fascination with trashy murder mystery shows and that Inferna liked comedies.

The dynamic we'd found made me happy, which meant I didn't feel bad about packing up a bag with some of my clothes and items to take to her place.

My apartment lease was up and maybe...

Maybe we would move in together.

Maybe it was too soon.

My stomach did a slow flip and I went up the stairs to the third floor, fishing out my keys from my pocket. The moment I put it in the lock, it felt like someone punched me in the gut.

I gasped and started to stumble backward, but then a figure slammed me against the wall with a snarl.

"*Witch*," they growled.

I shoved back, immediately calling on my magic. A spell left my lips, sending my assailant flying back.

I stumbled back again, breathing hard. My stomach still ached, my skin immediately coating in sweat. I looked up, realizing that they hadn't come alone.

Three creatures were moving towards me down the hall.

What the fuck?!

I threw up a blast of magic, feeling a bit of my energy leave me as I turned and took off running. I felt my bond to Inferna and Art tighten, and I pressed on it.

I didn't have time to call them. I didn't have time to text.

A growl behind me had me sidestepping just as a monster, most definitely a werewolf, tried to grab me. Their claws swiped out, their snarl chilling me to the bone.

My fucking leather oxfords weren't exactly good running material. I hit the second landing and then leapt over the side, using my magic to cushion my landing so my legs didn't snap as I hit the ground.

Pain ran through me, my body jarred by the impact.

Some witches were better at that type of magic, but at least I could do it.

I glanced behind me, which was a mistake.

A demon, one with flaking skin and three eyes, was

right behind me. Shadows shot out, curling around me like smoke.

I flicked my hand, sparks flying from my fingers. It was no use though, the moment his shadow touched me— I felt my magic drain immediately.

I fell to my knees, my breaths coming in painful gasps.

The demon chuckled. "No use fighting us, witch. You're coming with us."

"Why?" I rasped, shaking my head.

I was shivering now, prickles of fear piercing me.

Inferna and Art were all I could think about, along with my impending doom.

The demon waited for the other three creatures to catch up and I was immediately surrounded. I looked at their faces, realizing that one of them was actually a witch.

"You fucking Judas," I snarled at him, glaring.

He ignored me, his eyes flickering. He wore a long black cloak, one with a hood that hid most of his face.

I recognized him...

"Hazard?" I breathed, my lips parting.

"Let's get him out of here," Hazard growled.

Fuck. What was going on?

"I told you that you shouldn't have come," one of the creatures chuckled. "He now knows you're one of his betrayers."

Hazard ignored the demon. "Get him out of here, now. Take him to the basement."

The basement?!

"Why are you doing this?" I wheezed. "I'm no one. I've never done anything wrong. I come from good witches."

"You do come from good witches," Hazard growled. "Too good. We need omegas for breeding."

"Breeding?" I rasped, shaking my head. "You're out of your fucking mind, Hazard."

Hazard smirked, shrugging. "It's not my plan, anyway."

With that cryptic answer, he raised his hands. The ground lit up around us, a bright circle with symbols that raised up, floating around our group.

I tried to get up, but was immediately shoved back down to my knees. The wind picked up, howling as Hazard spoke a transportation spell.

We fell through the ground, straight through a portal. When we came out on the other side, I hit the ground hard — my head smacking concrete.

My vision started to swim, dotting in and out.

"Fuck," I gasped.

I could only make out the shape of cages and blurry faces before slipping out of consciousness.

CHAPTER NINETEEN
thursday

INFERNA

I felt my mating bond yanked tight, and then I felt his pain. I hunched over my desk with a pained gasp, fear running through me.

Calen was in trouble.

I clawed at my chest, panting as panic crept through me. I heard Art's worried cry, seeing him fly through our office doorway.

We came here early today, leaving Calen to run to his apartment for whatever he needed. Regret and guilt flooded me.

I knew people were after him.

"Where does he live?!" I snarled.

Art made a pained noise, coming straight to me. He grabbed my hand, dragging me into the middle of the office. His skin started to glow, his eyes lighting up like neon diamonds.

"If he's dead..." I started to say.

"Don't say that," Art snapped. "We'll get to him. Hold on to me, Inferna."

I did, wrapping my arms around his neck. A portal burned around us, one that had a much darker tint than the other we had taken together. Art pulled us through, darkness consuming us.

We landed in a parking lot and I turned just in time to see a group of demons disappear.

"FUCK!" Art shouted.

We both took off running, but we were too late.

They were gone.

I stared numbly at the ground, a chill working over my skin.

Art knelt down, running his fingers over the asphalt. He drew a symbol over the ground and it glowed red for a moment before snuffing out like a candle.

"Fucking hell," he growled, shaking his head.

"I'm going to slaughter every single one of them," I ground out.

"How?" Art asked, looking at me. "I can't put a tracker on the portal they just used. I have no idea where they went."

"What about our bond to Calen?" I asked, my hands curling into fists.

Art stared blankly for a moment and then stood up, pressing his lips together. He scowled. "Maybe."

"We have to try something," I whispered.

"I know, I know," he said, swallowing hard.

I hated feeling helpless. I hated—

"Hey," Art said, looking at me. "Stop it. I'm useless in a fight. You're useless with magic. We can help each other."

I let out a breath, fighting back tears. My chest hurt, the place where my bond to Calen resided feeling empty.

My witchling was in pain. He was scared and alone and...

"This is all my fault," I said.

"It's not," Art said. "And if it is, then it's mine too. The only thing I can think of right now is blood magic. I can't feel Calen's consciousness right now."

"I'll give you all my blood," I said, holding out my hand.

Art made a noise. "I swore I would never do this type of magic again."

I looked at him, my heart beating fast.

I could feel how conflicted he was. His eyes darkened, his lips pressing into a hard line.

"I don't know your past," I said, stepping closer to him. "I don't know your past, and I've only known you for a few days. But I know you are good, Art. And I don't think this would mean you are corrupt."

Art swallowed hard. "It's...it's addicting. And I'm good at it. It's powerful, and it's dark. It's what my coven was known for. But I would be able to find Calen."

"You can do it to me," I said. "I don't care. We have to find our mate. I can't think of another way."

"I can't either," he admitted. "I wish I could."

I leaned up, giving him a soft kiss. He took it and then pressed his forehead to mine.

"When we find him, I will be committing murder," I whispered. "So long as we're clear about who is corrupt here."

Art chuckled. "Sometimes murder is a little nice."

I smirked now, my tail flicking behind me. I took a step back and held out my hand.

Art winced, but he took my hand. "This might hurt a little, my love."

"I don't care. We have to find him."

Art nodded and dragged the tip of his finger over my wrist. It was like the blade of a knife and I sucked in a breath, watching as my blood welled.

Art leaned down, surprising me by dragging his tongue over the cut. It might have been erotic if we weren't doing this out of pure desperation.

His eyes lit up again, his aura of magic becoming even stronger. He made a dark noise, and when he looked at me — I remembered that witches were truly creatures too. He was feral, a low growl coming from him.

His lips parted and sparks came from his tongue, words leaving his mouth that I couldn't understand.

Fuck, I was kind of turned on by him like this.

My wrist started to sting, pain radiating up my arm. I made a little gasp as a circle burned around us, symbols drawing themselves in chaotic electric lines.

Art pulled me close to him as the air howled around us, shadows rising up. I closed my eyes as more pain stabbed through me, my blood feeling like it was boiling.

I still felt my bond to Art though, and even through the monstrous cloud that had overtaken him— I could feel him offering me comfort, trying to smother the pain.

I'm okay. Find Calen, I reminded him, pushing back.

He was reluctant, but the moment he gave in— the pain increased significantly. I let out a cry, my veins feeling like a thousand wasps were trapped inside. I held on to my mate, focusing on Calen. Calling to our mate.

The circle rose up and we fell through, tumbling through darkness. I closed my eyes, focusing on my breaths and on holding on to Art.

We came out on the other side, both landing on hard concrete. I lifted my eyes just in time to see two creatures rushing towards us.

Art groaned, now on his knees. His energy was somewhat depleted now, his glow disappearing.

Now, it was my turn.

I kicked off one of my heels, catching it in time to drive it straight through the head of a demon. He screeched as I shoved him back, raking my claws over his chest.

I let out a snarl, my wings bursting from my back.

The demon howled as another creature, a werewolf, ran straight for me. I kicked off my other heel, lunging forward and meeting him with full strength.

The fucker was strong, but I was determined. My tail whipped up, wrapping around his neck as I slammed him into a pole. He started to choke, shoving against me. I brought my knee up, hitting him right in his prized jewels.

He howled now too and I slammed him against the pole again. He passed out, slumping to the ground.

I turned, ready to fight again. I could feel one more presence, one that I couldn't see yet.

We were in a room, one with low ceilings. I glanced around wildly, horrified at what I was seeing.

Three of the walls were lined with cages, and within them were witches. Most of them were silent, unmoving.

I spotted my own and sucked in a breath. He was chained to the wall, his body naked and slumped to the side.

"Art," I called.

Art looked up, his expression changing. "LOOK OUT!"

Fuck. I spun just as a wall of shadows crashed down beside me. I dove out of the way, cursing under my breath.

Of course there was a fucking shadow demon here.

"Inferna," a gravely voice chuckled. "I should have known Dante's daughter would have been involved."

I turned to meet the demon's gaze. He had three eyes, a wall of darkness surrounding him.

"Who the fuck are you?" I growled.

"Someone who is not very fond of your family. They killed my vampire friend," he snapped.

"Sorry not sorry," I said, arching a brow. "I will end you, or you can leave. It's up to you."

"I think I can handle a fledgling succubus. You're not even one hundred yet," the demon chuckled.

I didn't like that answer. In fact, it pissed me off. Every now and then I would meet another demon and they would always laugh about me being a baby.

I wasn't a fucking baby. I was a grown ass woman and I was about to send this motherfucker back to hell for ever laying a hand on my mate.

"Fine then," I snarled.

The demon glared and then growled, baring rows of teeth at me.

He lunged for me and then I felt a presence behind me, one I recognized as Art. He stepped up next to me, throwing up a wall of light.

The demon howled and I used the moment to lunge forward, my wings giving me the speed I needed.

I didn't like killing and I remembered that as I drove my hand into one of his eyes. I felt the shadows engulf me, but they were weak and weren't taking my energy like they would have before.

"More light!" I yelled at Art.

Another wave of light flew up and the demon screamed. I shoved my hand in more, grimacing as his blood coated my skin. I yanked my hand back, jumping off him and hitting the ground next to my very tired, but amazing, witchy mate.

The two of us watched as the shadow demon stepped back, creating a little door of darkness and disappearing through it.

He wouldn't die, but...

"I thought you liked murder," Art breathed out with a chuckle.

"It's kind of gross," I admitted.

I looked around, still on edge. The werewolf was still passed out, and the other demon wasn't getting up. He wasn't dead, but he'd need time to recover.

I walked over to him, plucking my shoe from his head. I shook it off and then tossed it to the ground, sliding my foot into it. Art brought me my other one, kneeling down to slide it on.

I took a moment, arching a brow as he cradled my calf for a moment. He looked up, his eyes sparkling.

"You're magnificent, Inferna," he said, sliding my heel on.

I made a little growl. "And you're entirely too sexy, Art. Let's get our mate. And let's free these witches."

Art nodded, standing. We both looked around, the reality settling in.

This was horrific. This was like the things I'd heard murmurs about in regards to the past— a time when monsters and witches hated each other.

Why were these witches locked up?

"They're all spelled," Art said gruffly. "I can see the magical bonds. We need to get Calen out of here. And we will need to come back for the others."

"We can't leave them here," I hissed.

Art shook his head. "They aren't conscious. And we don't know how much time we have."

"I'm not leaving them behind," I snarled again, rushing across the room to our witchling.

I shoved open the door, the metal groaning under the strength of my grip. It buckled immediately and I stepped into the cage. Art rushed in after me, both of us kneeling next to Calen.

He wasn't moving. I pulled him into my lap, tears springing to my eyes.

I could feel his heart beating, hear his quiet breaths. Art raised his hands and there was that glow again. Calen made a little cry as magical bonds around his body ignited and then shattered.

His eyes flew open and he immediately sat up, panicking.

"Calen, Calen," Art said quickly.

I wrapped my arms around him, holding him. "Baby, we're here. We have you, my love. You're safe."

"You're safe," Art said, cupping his face.

Calen made a noise, a choked sob following it.

"I dont understand," he cried. "I don't understand what's happening."

"We don't either," Art said. "We don't either, but we're going to get out of here."

"We can't leave the others, Art," I whispered.

He met my gaze, his eyes flashing with worry. "Inferna, I am a witch. These are my own. But we will need to come back with better reinforcements."

Calen held on to both of us, letting out another sob.

"We have to come back immediately," I said.

Art nodded. "After our meeting. After we expose Claude and Alice. I have friends I can call."

"As do I," I said. "I'll rain hell on this place."

Art nodded again, and I felt the thrum of his magic. The

three of us were quickly pulled through a portal, and we landed in our office.

"I need clothes," Calen said, his voice eerily calm. "Also, Hazard was involved in this."

I winced.

"Hazard called in today," Art snarled, cursing under his breath. "Fuck. How many others were in on this, I wonder?"

"I don't know," I whispered. "I know no one here gets paid enough for this shit."

Calen snorted, leaning back against me.

"I always bring extra clothes," Art said. "Let me get them for you. We're not out of this yet."

"You've used a lot of magic," I said, watching as he wobbled when he stood.

Art waved his hand. "I'll be okay. I still have enough energy left."

Calen turned in my lap, wrapping his arms around me. I held him to me, closing my eyes for a moment.

"I was so scared," I whispered. "So scared."

"Me too," he murmured.

"We'll work through everything," I whispered softly. "It'll be hard to recover quickly."

He nodded. "Lots of cuddles and love."

"A ton of love," I agreed, looking up at Art as he brought clothes.

He was hanging on by a thread, one that was flimsy at best. Hell, we all were.

Still, I was already pulling myself together.

"How long do we have until the meeting?" I asked.

Art glanced up at a clock on the wall. "Office opens in twenty minutes. I'm sure they will be punctual."

I was most certain they would be, the bastards.

"Have you gotten a hold of Alex? Do you think he is in on this?"

Art swallowed hard. "I'm not sure, Inferna. This is a lot bigger than we know. I don't know much we can do, either. But, let me make some calls. We will save those witches after we handle Claude and Alice."

"Perfect," I said, already imagining how I was going to handle those two.

Come hell or high water, this meeting was going to be the end of their rule over Warts & Claws Inc.

CHAPTER TWENTY
meeting from hell

ART

The three of us were ready five minutes early. I had washed off the blood and dark magic from my hands, combed my hair, straightened my suit and tie.

I had called someone that I knew, and they were already headed towards the office. Inferna had phoned someone as well and it sounded like a whole fucking army was headed this way too.

Five minutes until 9 a.m.

I checked my phone.

Still no answer from Alex.

I was starting to think he was dead.

I let out a sigh, swallowing hard. My blood was still singing from the blood magic, the taste of Inferna on my tongue.

It was a magic I had sworn I would never touch again, but she had been right.

I had used it for good. I didn't feel as corrupt as I

believed I would.

Maybe it was how I used the magic that would make a difference.

I refused to be like those before me, but denying that part of me... denying that part of me suddenly felt foolish.

If I wasn't who I was, I wouldn't have been able to save my mate.

I looked over at Inferna and Calen. She had washed the blood off her skin, but not her heels.

She looked like she could rule all of heaven and hell.

I was a bit worried about Calen, but as Inferna said—we would cuddle and love each other after we escaped this nightmare.

"Ready?" I asked.

Inferna and Calen both nodded.

"Calen," I said. "You will stay hidden in here. I don't want Alice or Claude to know you have escaped. They may not realize that yet."

Calen nodded, gritting his teeth. "I want to fucking fight them."

"I know," Inferna said. "I know you do. But we need you here."

Calen nodded.

With that, I opened the office door, stepping out onto our floor. Some creatures and witches were already in, and all of their heads swiveled towards us.

Hazard was gone.

As was Poppins.

I wasn't the only one that noticed that, either.

Inferna made a noise. "Maybe it's a coincidence."

"Maybe," I whispered, but my stomach still twisted.

"Are you okay?" Lora asked us, her eyes wide.

"No," I said, clearing my throat. "No, we're not. But we will be."

I said that just as none other than Claude and Alice walked through the doorway, meeting my gaze from across the room.

"Good morning," I said, but the words most defitneily did not sound warm.

If good morning meant fuck you, then I had the right tone.

Alice grinned, gliding across the floor towards us. "Did dear Calen call in again?"

"He did," Inferna snapped.

She and I stood next to each other, a team against these two.

Claude studied us, narrowing his eyes. "I smell blood."

"Oh," Inferna said, grinning like the perfect professional she was. "I like to kill demons for breakfast," she said, smirking. "Specifically demons that like to kidnap witches."

Alice and Claude both stilled. Everyone in the room watched the exchange, gasps popping up here and there.

"I especially like killing demons that leave my mate naked and helpless in a cage. And I particularly like ending vampires that caused all of this," Inferna said, taking a step forward.

"You kidnapped witches?" Clay asked, stepping forward.

Lora also stepped forward, followed by a couple of our other employees.

Alice took a step back, glancing around the room. "One more step, and I'll have them kill Calen."

"Calen is safe, you blood sucking bitch," Inferna sneered.

Alice's eyes widened and Claude took a step back as

well. "I'll fucking end all of you," she said, but she sounded less sure than she had before.

A little less certain she could take on our office.

"You'll end us?" I laughed, stepping closer.

She and Claude stepped back, straight into a wall. Claude hissed, baring his fangs. "All of you will be fired for this!"

"I don't give a flying fuck," Mich growled.

There was a murmur of agreement and I was about to pounce forward, when a flash of light filled the room.

I turned, watching as a witch stepped out of a doorway of light.

Alex.

"Alex!" I yelled, shocked.

He barely acknowledged me, his eyes on Alice and Claude.

Claude and Alice looked like they were seeing a ghost.

"You're supposed to be dead!" Alice screamed.

Alex lifted his hands and a zap of lightning bolted through the room, staking both Alice and then Claude. Inferna and I stepped back, everyone yelling.

Claude and Alice both slumped to the floor.

Alex pulled on a set of leather gloves, his portal closing behind him. He then waved his hand and I watched in shock as the two of them turned to dust.

"Someone please call maintenance," Alex said stoically, turning to look at everyone. "It appears that some dust has piled up in our office."

I was in shock as much as everyone else. Alex arched a brow. "I said to call maintenance people. And go get some breakfast. I have some things to discuss with your bosses."

Lora and Mich were the only ones to linger for a moment, but then ultimately obeyed.

"We'll be okay," I said, giving a nod of assurance despite my voice shaking. "Go get some grub."

Inferna's hand slipped into mine and she gave it a hard squeeze.

Alex waited until everyone left and then sighed, his cold demeanor melting some.

"Fucking hell in a hand basket," he said. "This has been the week from hell."

"YOU'RE TELLING US!" Inferna yelled.

Alex shrugged, glancing at the pile of dust. "Betrayed by the vampire I did business with. Well, now he's out of commission for a bit and the contract states that I now own Claws Inc. Don't fuck me over," he mumbled, shaking his head.

"I've been trying to get a hold of you," I said, gaping at him.

"Well," Alex said, "let's go to the office. And let's go check on your mate. I already have witches heading to the basement."

"Basement?" I asked. "Is that where everything was happening?"

"Yes," Alex said. "That's where I was too, and luckily the two of you breaking in disrupted their magical wards. I'll explain myself."

Inferna snorted, shaking her head. "I can't believe any of this."

"It's been a strange time," Alex agreed.

The three of us went to the office and the moment I opened the door, Calen was throwing his arms around me. I picked him up immediately, carrying him over to my chair. I took a seat, still holding him to me.

Inferna came to my desk as well, sitting on the top.

Alex took her chair, unbuttoning his blazer as he took a seat.

"Monday, we all announced the merger," Alex said. "Claude and I had been talking about this for awhile and he convinced me that it was good timing. The moment the meeting ended, I was attacked by two witches and a few creatures. They took me to the basement below this building, trapping me against my will. I was unable to break free until the two of you came in. I'm not entirely sure what the motives were, but while I was there— I heard some talk. There is a group of witches and creatures working together, trying to find omegas so that they can create a new line of creatures. Like Alice, who is a vampire witch. It has been rare up until more recently to have a creature that can practice magic."

I let out a breath, rubbing Calen. He finally made a noise, turning in my lap so that he could look at Alex too.

"I just don't understand why this is suddenly happening," Inferna said.

Alex drummed his gloved fingers on the desk. "I dont know. But I do know, I can't run this company alone. And I would still like to run it with a creature."

Silence fell over the room and I found myself grinning. "Are you offering Inferna a position?"

"I might be," Alex said, arching a brow. "If she's interested. I think also, for the sake of...well, for the sake of what's going on, I'll buy back one of the floors we had and make it another office space. Inferna and I can have separate offices up there. Art, you would directly run the teams here. Calen, I don't know you."

Calen snorted, waving his hand. "I'm happy with where I'm at."

"Okay," Alex said. "Well, everyone will have tomorrow

off, paid. Everyone in the office. This week has been traumatic."

"It has been," I agreed, holding Calen a little tighter.

"And the omega witches were found?"

"They're being freed as we speak," Alex said. "I have a feeling I might hire a couple of them, to help them get back on their feet."

"We will need a proper HR department with free therapy," Inferna said sharply.

Alex's eyes glimmered a little. "So does that mean you accept?"

"Yes. So long as you understand that Art and Calen are my mates."

"Indeed," Alex said. "I don't really give two shits unless it becomes a problem."

"Okay then," Inferna said. "Then yes, I accept."

Calen and I both grinned, and finally relaxed a little.

Despite everything terrible that had happened, this week was still ending in a three day weekend with my two mates— and one of them just got a promotion.

"We also need to find Hazard," I said. "He betrayed us. He was in on it. And I suspect there are others."

Alex nodded, humming to himself. "I suspect so as well. But they will rat themselves out. For now, the immediate threat is over and everyone is safe. Also, for the sake of... legalities, we're going to wipe the record of this week. And we will pretend that I didn't just kill two vampires and that Inferna didn't maim three creatures earlier. We'll get better security too."

The three of us nodded, all agreeing.

"That was... powerful magic," I said warily.

Alex shrugged, standing. "I don't use it very often. As in, I never use it. I'm similar to you, Art, which is why I hired you. Bad covens, bad magic— but sometimes it comes in handy. I'll see the three of you Monday. Inferna, we'll go over your new role then. For now, try to get through the work day and then enjoy your time off."

"Thanks," we all said.

Alex raised his hand, created a portal, and then left us alone with a very surreal feeling.

"Well," Calen said, shaking his head. "I'm...sorry."

"For what?" I asked, laying my head against him.

Inferna came around the desk seating herself on top in front of us.

"I didn't know I would cause so much trouble," Calen whispered.

"You didn't cause any trouble," Inferna said, arching a brow. "Look at me. Both of you."

Both of our gazes snapped up, meeting hers.

"None of this was our fault," she whispered. "But we're all okay. I'm just thankful we're alive and can sit here together."

"Me too," Calen sighed. "Also, congratulations, Mistress."

"Yes," I said. "Boss. Now, you're really my boss."

"I am," she said, giving me a wicked grin.

"I think you might need to have a conversation with me in the bedroom," I said, smirking.

"I think I might need to have one with both of you," Inferna said, her tail sliding over. "Dinner, cuddles, and perhaps some knotting. I'd like to try some new things out."

"Like what?" Calen and I asked, both all too eager to hear what she had planned.

"Well, I have a flogger in my closet. Also, a whip and some collars," she said, smirking. "I kind of like the idea of collaring you both."

"I like that too," I whispered, feeling my cock starting to harden.

Calen wiggled in my lap on purpose, making me growl.

"Calen," I mumbled. "We're at work."

"That has yet to actually stop any of us," he chuckled.

"True," Inferna said, laughing. "Hmm. We'll save it for tonight. Let's go let everyone know about the three day weekend. Oh, and call maintenance, I guess."

I reached for my desk phone, dialing the number. Someone picked up and I cleared my throat. "Hi, there's some dust that came down on the floor from the air vents. Do you think someone can clean it up when there's time?"

"Of course," they answered. "We'll be there soon."

"Great," I said, hanging up.

I let out a sigh of relief.

We'd made it through the work week, and we're almost to our Friday.

CHAPTER TWENTY-ONE

CALEN

I woke up, ready to go to work, but then realized it was Friday and we had the day off.

Inferna moaned next to me, her hand sliding up my chest. "Back to sleep," she mumbled, nuzzling me.

Art was passed out to my left. His snoring would have kept Inferna and me up, but I used a little magic to silence the sound.

I relaxed, closing my eyes again.

Then, I realized I was hard.

I opened my eyes, peeking down.

Art had stollen the blankets from us, so I was completely exposed.

Fuck. I was super hard.

Inferna's breathing softened again as she fell back into a light sleep.

I fought off a moan, trying to close my eyes again, but... my cock pulsed, precum dripping from the tip. Morning wood was most definitely a thing, especially when I was sandwiched between my two mates.

I wiggled my hand free from Inferna, sliding it down to my cock. I gripped it just as she growled, raising her head. She glared through half lidded eyes, making a noise.

"I literally fucked you senseless last night," she mumbled. "Are you certain you're not an incubus?"

"I'm certain," I chuckled.

She smirked, her tail coming around and tracing up my leg. I sucked in a breath as she slapped my hand away, replacing it with her own.

Being an omega wasn't that bad, perhaps.

Inferna sat up and then straddled me, her body warm and soft against my own. I was even harder now that her breasts were in my face.

"Morning, witchling," she teased, leaning down.

I kissed her, groaning beneath her. Art stirred next to us and he let out a moan.

"Fuck, that's a hot thing to wake up to," he sighed happily.

"Get behind me," Inferna said. "I want to take both of you at the same time."

Art was up immediately. I thrust my hips up, rubbing the tip of my cock against her opening as he moved behind her.

"Morning, beautiful," he said, kissing her neck.

She moaned, tipping her head back. I leaned up, cupping one of her breasts and sucking her nipple.

Her gasp made me even harder.

Art ran his hands over her body, giving her little shocks here and there.

"Mmm, my wonderful mates," Inferna purred. "I want both of your cocks inside of me so badly."

"Yes, Mistress," Art groaned. "Anything you want."

"Anything," I agreed with a moan.

Inferna reached down, gripping my cock and slowly taking me. I groaned, pleasure burning through me as I slid inside of her. She took every inch, the ridges making her moan as she took them.

Art gripped her hips and I felt his cock against mine, the tip pressing. Inferna leaned forward with a gasp, and I gripped the blankets as he slowly worked his way into her.

"This feels so good," I gasped. "So fucking good."

Art grunted as he fit his cock in, ours rubbing together. Inferna gasped again, pressing her hands against my chest as Art began to slide back out.

He then thrust forward, the three of us crying out together.

"Fuck," I groaned.

Pleasure worked through me, our energy working together in tandem. I thrust up, enjoying both of their cries.

Art met my gaze over Inferna's shoulder, giving me a knowing smile. His hips pumped forward again, this time with a little more force.

I answered his thrust with my own, and within moments we found a rhythm that had our Mistress crying out.

Her nails raked over my skin and the nip of pain was enough the make me almost cum, but I held back.

She groaned. "Fuck, both of you feel so good."

Art began to thrust in and out harder, his head tipping back as he lost himself in pleasure.

"I'm so close," I gasped. "So close."

"I'm going to lock both of you inside of me," Inferna said, moving her hips.

We both fucked her harder, eager to be trapped inside

of her. The teeth felt good as they raked over our cocks, sending me spiraling even further.

"Cum inside me," she groaned. "I just want to be filled by both of you."

That was enough to make Art and me cry out. With one final thrust, Art's knot shoved inside, and we both started to cum. I could feel him against me, the heat of our cum filling her making me moan. I felt the teeth clamp around our cocks, around his knot.

I reached down, rubbing her clit in quick circles.

"Oh fuck!" she cried out.

I watched her cum, feeling her muscles contract around us.

Art and I both cursed, both reveling in the perfection of being together and being with Inferna.

She slumped forward, leaning against me. Art relaxed too, panting hard.

"I love you both," I whispered.

"I love you both too," Inferna said, making a happy hum in her throat.

"I also love you both," Art chuckled, letting out a pleased sigh. "I'm glad we have today off to just be together."

"Me too," I said, closing my eyes.

Yesterday had been an absolute nightmare, but even when I had been alone— I hadn't truly been alone.

I had felt Inferna and Art, even in the quiet darkness.

When Art had broken the binding spells, it had been like coming up from a heavy tide. I was thankful for both of them.

Monday, I had met my mates.

Tuesday, we had all made our mating bonds.

Wednesday, all hell had broken loose.

Thursday, we had survived a nightmare.

Friday... well. Thank goddess it was Friday. I was able to just lay in bed with my mates and feel...

Loved. Wanted.

Inferna gave me a gentle kiss and then melted back against me, sighing. "I'm going back to sleep while both of you are locked to me."

I nodded, yawning. "I think I can too."

Art snorted. "I'm going to stay up and then when I pull out, go make some breakfast. I'm thinking breakfast in bed sounds good."

"This *is* breakfast in bed," Inferna said.

I laughed and Art chuckled, giving her back a gentle rub. "This will include me dripping syrup on Calen and then licking it up."

"That sounds good," I groaned, my cock giving a pulse.

"Of course it does," Inferna teased, giving me a little love bite.

I grinned and closed my eyes again, letting out a deep breath. I was right where I wanted to be.

"Do you think other witches and monsters will date? Like within our office?" Art asked.

"Most definitely," Inferna said. "But, we don't need to think about anyone until Monday."

"Next week is a new week. But for now I just want to dream about your cocks inside of me and also figure out how we're going to have dinner with my family without the two of you losing a finger."

"Oh goddess," I moaned.

Art winced, making a face. "I'm sure it'll be fine. Just fine."

Inferna snorted, cuddling me. "I'm going back to sleep. I never sleep in."

"Yes, Mistress," Art chuckled, rubbing her.

He winked at me and I smiled, sinking back into sleep.

This week had been the longest week of my life, but it had also been the greatest.

"Go to sleep, witchling," Art said. "We have to rest up for meeting her family and for another Monday."

With that, I fell asleep with my monstrous Mistress and my bossy witch— knowing that this was the first of many sleepy, knotty mornings together.

horn-y resources department

HEAD OF HR

"We need another agent. One that they won't suspect. One that won't make the same mistakes," I growled.

"We have someone in mind. They're very good at what they do, sir. Very sneaky. Completely opposite of Alice."

"Is Alice truly dead?" I asked, drumming my claws on my desk.

"Yes," my secretary said.

"Ridiculous. I can't believe Alex escaped and then ended her. We're going to need someone that can sneak past him too. As well as the new Claws boss."

"Yes, sir. I'll send in the next agent. Don't worry sir, everything is still going to plan."

I waved a hand at her, growling. She scurried off, leaving me to glare. I stood up, walking over to my window. I could see the Warts & Claws building from here, could see the front doors perfectly.

I could see when employees left and when they returned.

Always watching. Waiting.

Everything was going according to plan, even though two of my pawns had been eliminated.

Monday would be a whole new chess board, and I already had the upper hand.

It was a game I liked playing.

One that I would always win.

clio's creatures

Hello Creatures 🎃

My name is Clio Evans and I am so excited to introduce myself to you! I'm a lover of all things that go bump in the night 👻, fancy peens 🥒, coffee ☕, and chocolate 😈

IF you had the chance to be matched with a monster- what kind would you choose?!

Let me know by joining me on FB and Instagram. I'm a sucker for werewolves to this day 🐺💀

P.S.

Join my Newsletter by clicking here- I won't spam you, but I will offer you fun rewards for being one of my monster loving creatures.

Clio's Creature Newsletter

thank you

To Erica Cooke— for being my amazing editor. Thank you for being a wonderful friend and for your support on this monster filled adventure. Also, thank you Morris for always being my first reader. Love you!

Also to work culture— you nearly had me and I'm glad I escaped ;)

also by clio evans

Creature Cafe Series
Little Slice of Hell

Little Sip of Sin

Little Lick of Lust

Little Shock of Hate

Little Piece of Sass

Little Song of Pain

Little Taste of Need

Little Risk of Fall

Little Wings of Fate

Little Souls of Fire

Little Kiss of Snow: A Creature Cafe Christmas Anthology

Warts & Claws Inc. Series
Not So Kind Regards

Not So Best Wishes

Not So Thanks in Advance

Not So Yours Truly

Not So Sincerely

Printed in Great Britain
by Amazon